STEAM

HANDLERS: BOOK 1

LYNN TYLER

Lynn Tyler Books
http://lynntylerbooks.com

Lynn Tyler Books
http://lynntylerbooks.com

Publisher's Note: This is a work of fiction. Names, characters,
places, and incidents are a product of the author's imagination.
Locales and public names are sometimes used for atmospheric
purposes. Any resemblance to actual people, living or dead, or
to businesses, companies, events, institutions, or locales is completely coincidental.

Book Layout © 2015 BookDesignTemplates.com

Steam/Lynn Tyler. – 2nd ed.
ISBN 978-0-9951899-6-6

To my 5th grade teacher, Mr. Tarn, who taught me to never give up.

CONTENTS

Chapter One

Sloan Shirer laughed at the sight his wife, Dara, made dancing in the rain, arms spread out and face tilted skyward. "It's beautiful, Sloan," she called, twirling around.

"You're beautiful," he called back. He made the drops swirl around her, just to hear her laugh.

"Sloan," Raven shouted. "I'm glad you're having fun, but we're training."

Dara giggled and pointed at Sloan. "Yeah, Sloan. You're supposed to be training," she teased.

He stuck out his tongue at his wife and focused on his task again. As the water handler for the MacAlister clan, the water was his to manipulate to his liking. If he wanted to create a whirlpool in a pond, it was easily done. If he wanted to manipulate a lake into one giant wave, he could. And if he wanted to create the perfect storm, he could.

Well, maybe he couldn't create the perfect storm on his own. But if he combined his magic with the magic of the clan's three other handlers, they could do just about everything. "Anna," he called. "Can you increase the wind?"

He couldn't hear her response, but her husband, Addison, flashed him a thumbs up. It took a few minutes before he felt the breeze increase and a quick glance in the air handler's direction showed him she concentrated fiercely. Her intense focus didn't surprise him. Anna had only come into her magic a couple of years ago and was still learning how to manipulate it to her liking.

As soon as his magic collided with Anna's the intensity of the storm increased until it raged around them.

Raven, the MacAlister clan leader, appeared in front of him. "You're doing well, Sloan. The dragons are impressed."

Sloan felt his chest puff out. The dragon queen, her son, and a small contingent of their guards had joined them that morning. They had been allied with the dragons for a few years and their queen seemed to be fascinated with their magic. Her son, Prince Gareth, was her second in command, and had taken to accompanying her on her visits. To be complimented by such ancient beings was a huge honor.

Once the storm was sufficiently large enough, it was time for the other handlers to join in. The earth handler added her power first, making the ground rumble and shake under their feet. She was skilled enough to stop the ground from shifting under his feet and he smiled his thanks at her.

The fire handler shot a stream of fire directly into the heart of the storm, heating the rain until it exploded into a boiling downpour. "That would cook anyone who wandered by," Sloan shouted with glee.

He wasn't bloodthirsty. He didn't want to kill any innocents. But the tensions between the MacAlister clan and the Keita and Takahashi clans, the two other witch clans, were increasing at a rapid pace. The handlers had to get their powers in sync or risk heavy casualties when the battle finally broke out between the three clans.

Leith MacAlister paced the perimeter of the storm anxiously. His long blond hair whipped around his face and his mouth was turned down in a frown. It wasn't unusual for Leith to be frowning. In fact, Sloan sometimes thought Leith's face would crack if he tried to smile. The pacing, however, was unusual.

He didn't have a chance to ask Leith what was wrong though. It was getting harder to control his magic now that the three other handlers had mingled their powers with his.

Cupping his hands, he began shaping the rain into a water funnel. If he could master holding the water funnel during a storm of this proportion, he could do anything. Anna's magic tugged against his before merging with it.

The sensation of combining their magics was mildly unpleasant. The power buzzed up his arms, adding to the strength of his own magic until it was almost impossible to hold, but it wasn't the most uncomfortable thing about the whole experience. For some reason, every time he succeeded in joining his magic with that of another handler, all his walls seemed to fall away. He could feel Anna's presence in the back of his mind, like a silent observer to his every thought and emotion.

Of course, it went both ways. Once they'd established their connection, he could clearly see her determination to create the storm. He knew she feared they'd fail and disappoint the clan. Her nervousness of performing such a feat in front of spectators was so acute, he could have sworn it was his own feeling.

He tried his very best to remain ignorant to any of her feelings that weren't relevant to what they were doing, but apparently, she and Addison had had a particularly satisfying night in bed.

Barely keeping the amused grin off his face, he concentrated on the task at hand. The addition of the wind created a funnel more massive than he had expected. "Awesome!" he shouted.

Raven and Leith started waving their arms in the air. He could see their mouths moving, but the wind whisked their words away. It looked like they wanted the handlers to end the storm.

It was easier said than done. Pulling back that amount of magic into his body would be excruciating. He resigned himself to an uncomfortable evening and started absorbing his power into his very cells.

It was slow going. The earth handler had ceased the earthquake and the fire handler had extinguished the flames. It would be harder for him and Anna to stop their storm, since their magic had been let out a lot more.

Finally, he had the rain slowed to a drizzle. He looked around for his leader to question the sudden decision and was confronted with his worst nightmare.

The ground was stained with blood. Raven, Leith and the other handlers were surrounded by the enemy and were engaged in a battle to save their own lives.

Everywhere he looked, there was another Takahashi or Keita witch or one of their allies. Werewolves were snapping their jaws and lunging at everyone they considered an enemy, and vampires were busy tearing out people's throats.

How had the other clans figured out what they were doing?

He summoned a single, massive jet of water and used it to knock a werewolf off Raven and a vampire away from Leith. He swiveled his head around frantically, searching for Dara in the chaos. All he could see was Anna, who had conjured a funnel cloud to blow the other witches, werewolves, and vampires away from the MacAlister clan.

The dragons had shifted and clawed at the vampires, who seemed to be concentrating their attacks on them, blowing fire at them.

He sent another jet of water out, this time directly at a Takahashi handler, who hurled boulders left, right and center.

A searing pain shot through him and he collapsed, landing on his hands and knees. He struggled to his feet and had almost made it when another lightning shaft of agony bolted through his system, followed by an empty chasm in his soul. He'd never experienced something like this personally, but he'd heard whispers about it from the earth and fire handler. Just as he had felt Anna come into her magic two years ago, he keenly felt the death of at least two of the MacAlister handlers.

Fighting through the pain, he forced himself to his feet and noticed the wind still blew. Anna must be alive. Which meant the earth handler and the fire handler were dead, their magic now transferred to two unborn MacAlister children.

They were hopelessly outnumbered, and now that two of their handlers were gone, they didn't have much hope of surviving the battle. He hoped Raven had enough time to get back to clan grounds and set the evacuation plan in place. If he didn't give the order for the clan to disperse, they would be easier to kill than fish in a barrel. The clan would be decimated.

He shook his head, trying to clear it of the lingering pain, and focused on drawing up as much water from the soil as possible. Maybe he could create a giant wave and flood the attackers out.

A scream pierced the air, and Sloan spun around to find Anna kneeling on the ground. He made a mad dash for her. If the MacAlisters had any hope of surviving at all, they needed both him and Anna. They couldn't be down three handlers. It wasn't until he skidded to a halt next to the fallen handler that he realized she wasn't screaming because she was hurt.

The air handler cradled her husband's head in her lap. Addison's eyes were open but his stare was empty. Blood trickled from both his nose and his ears. Sloan pawed at the man's neck, searching for a pulse. "It's no use," Anna said in a dead voice. "I turned around and he was holding his head before he collapsed. It had to one of the damn Takahashi handlers. One of them must have gotten into his head when I wasn't paying attention."

Sloan bent over the fallen witch. His pupils were blown wide and the whites of his eyes were bloodied. It certainly looked like a psychic attack.

"When I started running toward him, I blinked and realized I was back where I started. The Keita handlers stole some time from us."

Fuck. It was no secret the Keita clan handlers could manipulate time. If they had reversed time, even for a few seconds, there was no telling what had happened. Everything he remembered from the past few minutes could actually never have happened. He needed to find his wife.

The battle still raged around him, but Sloan risked a quick glance around, locating Dara, who was using her magic to strengthen Raven's.

Reassured, he turned back to Anna, only to find her pressing a kiss to her dead husband's forehead. She eased him to the ground and rose to her feet. Her eyes flashed and the wind increased dramatically. Suddenly, a funnel cloud appeared. Anna screamed, a sound of pure fury, and sent the tornado racing toward the Takahashis.

Sloan watched for a few seconds, stunned by the sheer power behind the wind funnel, before spinning around to run to Dara. She could help him bolster his magic so he could wash these fuckers away.

In a frantic attempt to locate her, Sloan eased up on the rain and strained his eyes.

His heart stopped when he finally caught sight of Dara again, in time to see a Takahashi witch wave his hand and a massive boulder go flying toward his wife.

He screamed for Anna to blow the boulder off its deadly course, but it was too late. It crashed into her, knocking her to the ground and crushing her under its weight.

His heart was trying to pound its way out of his chest by the time he stumbled to a stop next to his wife. He redirected his water jet and managed to push the boulder off Dara but she didn't move. Instinctively, he knew she was already gone.

A different kind of pain, not physical but still as potent, hit him and he dropped to his knees and examined her. He couldn't bring himself to look at her abdomen, which was surely mangled beyond belief. There was no way she could have survived, but he searched for a pulse anyway. Nothing.

Desperate for any thread of hope, Sloan threw up a wall of water to surround them and shuffled to her side, ready to administer CPR.

He regretted his actions as soon as he pressed his palms to her chest and his hands sank farther into her flesh than they ever should have.

There wasn't even a word to describe the murderous wrath that swamped him. Letting the wall drop, Sloan surged to his feet and threw his arms in the air. He didn't even attempt to control his magic. Instead, he let it flow unchecked, allowing it to grow and evolve, until it seemed to have a life of its own.

His magic collided suddenly with Anna's. The resulting storm was truly terrifying but he didn't care. He had enough sense in the face of his grief to make sure none of his own clan were harmed. Anna seemed to have the same thought because Raven and Leith were only damp and relatively unruffled.

When it was over, there was no sign of either the Takahashi or the Keita clans, or their allies. The dragons were gone too, but that didn't really faze him.

Knees buckling, Sloan sank to his knees as grief overwhelmed him. He gathered Dara's broken body in his arms and buried his face in her hair. Anna sobbed somewhere nearby, and he could make out Leith's voice as he spoke lowly to her.

Raven sat down next to him and Sloan lifted his head. Tears were streaming down his leader's cheeks. "Come on, Sloan. We need to get back to the castle. We have to give the evacuation order."

But Sloan didn't care. He didn't care about the two dead handlers, his mourning leader or even Anna, who was still crying for her husband. He didn't care about separating the clan they worked so hard to bond or the fact that they had to wait twenty-five years before the new handlers would come into their magic.

All he cared about was his wife, now dead, and the sucking wound her death left in his chest where his heart should be.

Chapter Two

Sloan stared down at his plate and made a face. Raven should really think about ordering out for a pizza once in a while. Seriously, why did they need to have some kind of roast meat, potatoes and gravy every night?

"Everything all right, Sloan?"

The sound of his leader's voice had Sloan looking up. He was so goddamned sick of that question. He hadn't been remotely all right since the day he'd lost Dara, twenty-five years ago. "I'm fine," he said tonelessly.

Raven raised one eyebrow but didn't comment any further. At least, he didn't comment on Sloan's attitude. Instead, he went back to the conversation he'd been having with Leith before he'd evidently seen Sloan sticking his tongue out at his dinner. "I haven't had much luck in tracking the dragons down. I don't know where else to look. Any advice, Leith?"

The blond giant leaned forward, and Sloan barely covered his snort with a cough. He knew exactly what Leith was about to say. Then again, Leith's replies never changed much. "I'm a Seeker, Raven. I sense and find magic. I don't track down huge, scaly lizards."

"You haven't had much luck seeking out any of our missing handlers either," Sloan muttered.

Sloan knew he was playing with fire. No one messed with Leith. The witch was the oldest in their clan, five hundred years old if the rumors could be believed, and he was from a different time. One where an insult like the one Sloan had given him could be resolved in a fight to the death.

He tensed, waiting for the blow, but it never came. Leith merely ignored him and continued with his statement. "However," he said without even a glance in Sloan's direction, "I would suggest searching the cliffs. If the dragons have taken to their natural form instead of their human form, they're probably lodged in one of the larger caverns."

Bored with the whole thing, Sloan started twirling his finger in the air. Instantly, a water funnel rose from his goblet and he sent it on a mini rampage across the table. His magic simmered through him and he rolled his head, trying to release some of the buildup. The waterspout sucked up the liquid from every goblet on the table, growing larger and larger with every passing second.

The trick wasn't releasing enough of the power and the magical overload was starting to make him a little jumpy. He knew from experience if he didn't find an outlet soon, it would feel like he was being flayed alive.

Of course, the easiest answer would be to head out to the training fields Raven had set up for the handlers and direct his energy into the pond. But he itched for a fight.

Sending the funnel higher into the air, he made it hover over his leader's head. A mixture of water, wine and juice swirled over Raven's shaggy black hair. All he needed to do was let it go and it would drench the man. Raven would then launch himself across the table and Sloan would have the fist fight he was looking for.

Raven, however, seemed to have other ideas. "Sloan, I suggest you fly that spout out the window before letting it go."

"And if I don't?" Sloan asked, trying to inject as much insolence into his tone as possible.

"I will prevent you from using any magic for a week."

Sloan's jaw dropped and he nearly lost control of the

funnel. It wavered dangerously above Raven's head before Sloan sent it out the open window. As the MacAlister clan leader, Raven was the only witch who had the power to prevent him from using his magic. If he thought not being able to dissipate his magic was uncomfortable now, it would be excruciating after seven days. "Geez," he muttered. "I'm just trying to lighten things up."

Anna, who had been watching the whole thing through wide eyes, shook her head. "You're out of control, Sloan."

He opened his mouth to shoot back a verbal dagger when he saw the look in her eyes. She seemed horrified by Raven's threat. Then again, as the air handler, she would know exactly what he was going through. Hell, she was probably as uncomfortable as he was.

Shoving a piece of meat in his mouth, he chewed and swallowed, determined to ignore the way it melted on his tongue or how the rich gravy felt like velvet sliding down his throat. He wasn't in the mood to find anything remotely pleasant.

He turned to Raven instead, trying to redirect the conversation to something a little less volatile. "Why do you want to get back into contact with the dragons, anyway?"

Ever the gentleman, Raven wiped his mouth with a linen napkin before answering. "You know the prophecy, Sloan. The war to end all wars is coming. It behooves us to have as many people on our side when it happens. The dragons aligned with us the last time, so it stands to reason that they may wish to ally with us again. We can't take any chances since the last time, the Takahashis were allied with the werewolves and the Keitas with the vampires."

This time, Sloan didn't even bother to hide his snort

of derision. "Do you still believe in that prophecy?"

Raven raised his eyebrows again and looked at him with curiosity. "You don't?"

Summoning a stream of water from the pitcher in the middle of his table and directing it into his goblet, Sloan thought about the best way to word his answer. Despite Sloan's current mood, Raven was a good man and deserved a good amount of respect. "No, I don't believe in the prophecy."

"Why?" Leith's deep voice cut through the awkward silence his declaration had caused.

Surprised, Sloan turned to Leith. The man rarely spoke unless he was asked a direct question. Leith gazed at him with interest, almost like he was some science experiment gone wrong.

Sloan squirmed in his chair a little, uncomfortable with the stares he was getting from the three other witches. "Well, the prophecy also says each handler will go to battle with their soul mate by their side. How is it possible for me to go into that battle with my soul mate when Dara died in the last battle twenty-five years ago?"

He focused on his plate, unable to look anyone in the face. He couldn't stand to see the pity he knew would be there.

The silence that settled over the room was smothering and he took a sip of water to try and ease his throat.

Finally, Anna spoke in her gentlest voice. The one she usually reserved for children and scared kittens. "Is it possible that Dara wasn't your soul mate?"

Rage swamped him and he shot up from his chair, pointing at Anna. "How dare you?" he accused. "How dare you question my love for my dead wife? How would you feel if I questioned your feelings for Addison?"

Somehow Raven had made it across the room before Sloan even noticed he'd moved. One of Raven's arms came across his chest and the other draped around his middle, like a father hugging his child from behind. "That's not what she meant and you know it," he whispered in Sloan's ear.

The anger drained out of him as fast as it had boiled over, leaving him feeling guiltier than hell. "I know. I'm sorry, Anna. What I said was uncalled for."

A brisk breeze swept through the room, reminding them all that, although Anna was better at restraining herself than Sloan, she could have taken him on in an instant. There were tears in her eyes though. Sloan's mood sank to a new low, knowing he'd caused Anna to remember her own lost love.

She nodded but the breeze didn't stop, and it combined with Sloan's power to form a small rainstorm, complete with miniature forks of lightning. It wasn't unusual for them to create tiny storms inside. It was almost like, with the absence of the other two handlers, he and Anna were missing some kind of anchor. He only barely hung on to control of his magic at the best of times. The accidental collision of their powers was almost too hard to handle.

Raven pushed Sloan down until his butt planted firmly in the chair. "Calm down, both of you, before you cause a damn hurricane."

With a lot of concentration, Sloan pulled the magic back into himself. He shivered at the unpleasant sensation and saw Anna doing the same. That was the thing with magic. Once released, it really didn't like being pulled back in. Pushing his plate away, he rose from his chair once more. "I'm not hungry. I need to go practice or something before I jump out of my skin."

Raven pushed him down once more and replaced the plate. "You need to eat more. You've lost too much weight."

There was no use arguing with the leader. Once he'd made his mind up, it took an act of God to change it. Sloan closed his eyes and rubbed his throbbing temples. He really needed to get to the pond and release some of this build up before he ended up flooding the dining room, and then go to bed. Maybe he should sleep for the next decade. Maybe then, the pain wouldn't be so bad.

"I know," Anna whispered from beside him.

He opened his eyes to see her kneeling at his side. She took one of his hands in both of hers. "I know it hurts. And I know you feel like you should have died instead of Dara. But that's not what happened. You're here, but you're only going through the motions of living. We need you to actually give a shit if any of us are going to survive the coming war."

There wasn't even time for Sloan to question the damn prophecy again.

Leith, who had been motionless the entire time, sat straight up in his chair, his eyes wide with wonder. "The fire handler ... has come into magic."

Raven rushed over to his seat, where his cell phone was lying on the table. He started dialing even as he barked orders. "Leith, take Matthew with you on your search. He can help navigate the human society. Matthew?" he said into the phone.

A surge of power ran through Sloan, electrifying his senses and sensitizing his body in a way it hadn't been stimulated in twenty-five years.

Sloan had only experienced it once in his life, when Anna had come into her powers. This time, the sensation was shockingly different. His cock swelled in seconds, and he pushed Anna away gently, embarrassed by his body's response to the new handler magic.

He shivered and looked at Raven, who looked shaken.

"She's so strong," Raven muttered.

Feminine power. Of course. Now that Sloan had clued into it, he could taste the vanilla and cinnamon of female magic on his tongue. No wonder his body had responded.

Raven took a breath and adjusted his belt. Sloan knew the feeling. He was kind of afraid his dick would break off if he tried to stand up. "Find her fast," the leader said to Leith. "There's no way the Takahashi or Keita seekers missed the power surge. Find her before they do. And watch out for hunters."

Another wave of power rushed over Sloan, and every muscle in his body locked as he barely prevented himself from ejaculating in his pants.

Finally, things seemed to settle down a little and he tried not to blush. He hadn't felt the need to orgasm when Anna had come into her magic but he'd been told it was different each time. The new magic pushing at them didn't dissipate, but his body gradually grew used to the sensation.

Raven rushed around, talking about adding a fire pit to the training fields. "Anna, Sloan, be prepared to train her."

Great. The last thing Sloan needed was to train a new handler in how to control her magic. Especially one who affected him like this.

Chapter Three

"I'm leaving for the day," Sunny said to three of her co-workers. The women were all gathered around a computer screen, ogling a half-naked male model.

"God, I love my job," one of them said with a sigh. "Every morning I wake up dreading coming to work and having to deal with the fashion editor from hell. Then I remember I get to ogle men like that every day, and I remember why I haven't quit yet." She pointed to the model, clad only in a pair of boxer briefs and a smile, and sighed.

Sunny giggled. She liked her job for more than the male models, but she had to admit they did make things a little more interesting. "They do break up the day," she replied.

Another one of her co-workers sighed dramatically and turned off the screen. "Why can't my boyfriend look like that?"

Shaking her head, Sunny pointed at the woman and smiled. "Don't complain. I've seen the flowers he sends you every Friday."

"Yeah. He's pretty great. He's out for the night though. Are you sure you don't want to join us for drinks tonight? I'll even treat you, since it's your birthday."

It was tempting. It wasn't like she had anything else waiting for her at home. But Sunny shook her head again. No matter how long she'd held this job, she still couldn't get past the idea that if she got close to someone, she would have to leave them behind. It was how she'd lived her entire life. "Maybe next time," she said instead.

"We're going to hold you to that." Sunny giggled again

as the women reached behind the screen and extracted a box. She recognized it as a pastry box from the local bakery. "Anyway, we wanted to give this to you. Happy Birthday. Enjoy it with a glass of wine and a bubble bath. You only turn twenty-five once, you know."

Touched, Sunny accepted the box. "Thanks. I will." She looked around, a little embarrassed. She didn't quite know how to act around people these days. "You guys have a good time tonight. I'll see you on Monday."

All three women nodded. "Thank goodness for weekends," one of them said. "It gives me two entire days to recover from Friday night. You promise you'll join us soon?"

"Maybe next week," Sunny replied, a little cornered. She wasn't certain how she felt. She wanted so badly to throw away all of her reservations and foster some real friendships.

Maybe the fact that she'd been at the magazine for more than a year meant she could actually make some friends. She'd never been anywhere longer than a year before. Even the foster families she'd grown up with had usually given up on her after about eight months and she was shunted to another family.

With her brain racing, she waved good-bye and headed out to her car. Unlocking the door, she slid into the driver's seat and carefully placed the pastry box on the passenger seat.

She stroked the steering wheel affectionately. The car was more than just a car to her. It was the first thing she'd ever purchased. It was the only thing she'd had for longer than five years. Hell, it was the only thing she'd had for longer than two years; although, this job was approaching the eighteen-month mark. Regardless, the car was almost like a child to her.

She drove the twenty minutes to her apartment building and hopped out, making sure to lock the doors behind her. She lived in a fairly safe neighborhood and there were lights in the parking lot, but one could never be too careful.

Letting herself into the building, Sunny bypassed the elevators and burst through the stairwell door. The past few weeks had been strange. She was losing weight left, right, and center no matter how much she ate. It seemed like her metabolism had been ratcheted up by ten levels.

The amount of energy she had was outrageous. She lived on the sixth floor, and she'd been literally sprinting up the stairs every day for a week. She'd been hitting the gym like a maniac too, running on the treadmill until the person behind her started to get frustrated with her hogging the machine. Then, she'd move onto the stationary bike and hit the weights until her muscles screamed. It didn't matter what she did. She still felt restless and twitchy.

Maybe her co-workers were right. A glass of wine and a bubble bath might actually relax her enough to lull her to sleep tonight.

But first, she wanted to peek inside the box. The bakery was well known for having the best pastries, and she'd been drooling over the window displays every day.

She slowly opened the box, pausing halfway to savor the rich scent of chocolate wafting from the cardboard container. She loved chocolate almost as much as she loved her car. Closing her eyes, she tried to picture what treat her co-workers had bought for her. A brownie? A slab of fudge?

Finally giving in, Sunny opened her eyes and finished tearing into the box. Inside sat a beautiful chocolate cupcake.

Only one thought ran through her head. *Yum.*

She pulled the cupcake out of the box and placed it on a little plate before rooting around in a kitchen drawer. She had to have a birthday candle in here somewhere. She loved candles and had them stashed all over the place.

A little pink one caught her attention and she stuck it in the center of the cupcake. She lit it and stared at the tiny orange flame. Shivers raced down her spine and something deep inside her tugged toward the fire. The pull toward the flame was so intense, it was almost creepy.

Closing her eyes, she did the same thing she did every year on her birthday. She sang "Happy Birthday" to herself and blew out the candle, prepared to make some silly wish.

Except this time, unlike other years, the flame didn't extinguish.

Instead, it looked a little bigger and seemed to glow a little brighter.

Sunny was pretty sure she didn't have any trick candles hanging around. There was no reason for the flame to continue to burn.

Electricity crackled along her skin, goose bumps breaking out over her entire body. Something big grew inside her. It was almost like her body was building up for some kind of huge event. She'd gone from feeling twitchy and restless to feeling like her skin was about to split wide open. It was excruciating and thrilling all at once. The fire fascinated her, drawing her closer like the proverbial moth to the flame.

The flame grew bigger and bigger until the entire cupcake was engulfed. If she didn't blow it out, it was going to set her table on fire. Ignoring the fact that her body was about to explode, Sunny bent over and blew at the candle again, putting all the extra energy she could behind it.

It was almost like she'd thrown a jug of gasoline around the room, soaking the carpet and walls, the fire burned so big and so fast. Within seconds, the entire apartment was on fire. She rushed for her fire extinguisher but it was too late. The fire alarms were already going off in the hall and she could hear the faint sound of sirens outside.

Shit, shit, *shit*. What the fuck had happened?

* * * *

Two weeks later, Sunny was still staying in her cheap motel room. Her apartment building had completely gone up in flames. The fire chief had made a statement to the press about how he'd never seen a building burn down so fast. According to him, it was like the fire had had a life of its own. When they'd sprayed the building with water, it had seemed like the flame would jump out of the way.

Something told her not to come forward with her story of creating the fire. For one, she really didn't feel like having another stay in a psychiatric unit. One stay as a teenager had been enough, thank you very much. And she was pretty sure if she told the chief about how the flame had responded to her, they would lock her back up faster than she could say "Bob's your uncle."

But there was something else holding her back from coming forward with her story. It was some strange sense of self preservation. It was almost like a fight or flight response. Maybe it was the fact that there seemed to be an awful lot of strangers hanging around her these days. Strangers who stared at her shrewdly. People who liked to pat down their waistband when they noticed her watching, like they were reassuring themselves their protection was still in place.

Maybe she *should* check herself into the psych unit after all.

Of course, things always had a way of going from bad to worse. Strangely, the pressure which had been building in her had disappeared after the fire and had stayed dormant for a couple of days. But it didn't stay that way. The restless sensation came significantly more often after the fire. It was like something was building inside her, growing until it was too large to be contained by her body. Sometimes she felt like clawing at her skin in a desperate attempt to release some of the pressure.

Add that to the fact that every time she experienced a strong emotion, fires broke out around her, and she seriously considered investing in a fire extinguisher manufacturer. She didn't have to be angry to have a fire start. No, she could be sad, happy, whatever. Hell, even getting aroused was a no-no.

At first, no one had made the connection between her and the fires. It wasn't like anyone had witnessed her strolling over to a wastebasket and dropping in a flaming match. In fact, many times, other people would be talking with her and the fire would start on the other side of the room.

But it wasn't long before people started to notice she happened to be in the room each and every time a fire started.

Now, she sat in her motel room after being fired. Her employer had no evidence to actually press charges against her, but the fact that the fires only happened when she was present was enough for them to release her from her contract. And all of her previously supportive co-workers, the same ones who had invited her out for drinks a few short weeks ago, avoided her like the plague.

She was at a complete loss as to what to do. She had

no job, no home and no possessions, save for her car. She'd like to think she'd been in worse positions before, but she really hadn't. She'd always figured something out before, but she needed to wallow in self-pity a little, even if it was only for a few minutes.

Grabbing the chocolate bar she'd purchased on the way here, she unwrapped it and took a huge bite. Chocolate always made things better. Well, bearable, anyway.

Lying back on the lumpy mattress, she closed her eyes and munched, wishing someone would knock on her door with the answer to all her problems.

Suddenly, there was a hard thumping against her door, like someone was pummeling it with a fist.

Her eyes flew open and she sat up so fast, her head spun.

Somehow, she doubted it was her fairy godmother knocking.

Chapter Four

Sunny tried looking through the peephole, but for some reason, it had completely clouded over. She made a mental note to speak to the motel management about fixing it as she slid the chain lock into place and opened the door wide enough to look outside.

Two men stood there, staring back at her. They were both blond, but that's where the resemblance ended. The guy on the right was of average height but had an absolutely fabulous body. His white dress shirt clung to him like a second skin and his gray slacks molded to his thighs perfectly. He had a friendly smile and pretty blue eyes.

The man next to him scared the bejeezus out of her. He was huge. Mountain like, even. His white-blond hair was tied back in a ponytail that hung nearly to his waist and his shoulders were nearly as wide as the door frame. But his eyes frightened her the most. They were gunmetal gray and seemed bottomless. She had a fleeting thought that if she stared at his eyes long enough, she would get lost in them. And not in the good, romantic kind of way, either.

Faced with such an intimidation, Sunny did the same thing she always did when she felt backed into a corner. She got lippy. "What do you want?"

The words sounded rather flippant, even to her.

The shorter man smiled again and shuffled over so he was directly in her view. "Hi. My name is Matthew Samuels and this is Leith MacAlister. Can we come in and speak with you for a few minutes?"

The soft, Australian accent probably had the girls falling at the guy's feet. Not her though. As attractive as this

Matthew was, Sunny had always been drawn to the more tall, dark and handsome type. "No, I'm fine. Good-bye."

Her attempt to close the door was thwarted when the big guy slapped his hand against it and used brute strength to keep it open. "Actually, it is not a request, Ms. Kerrigan."

"And my answer isn't negotiable. Good-bye," she said. Somehow, it didn't surprise her that they knew her name.

Leith tried to force the door open. Luckily, the chain held but the door frame creaked under the pressure. "We have information you might find helpful, Ms. Kerrigan. About what's happening to you. And about your parents."

The mention of her parents that gave her a second's pause. Her parents had been killed when she was a baby. She'd read the police report on her eighteenth birthday. The lead detective had stated he suspected her parents had been victims of a drive-by shooting. But the medical examiner hadn't found an exit wound or bullets on either of her parents.

Despite her desire to know more about her parents, she wasn't stupid. She realized she only had a few seconds to act when she saw Leith's fingers wrap around the edge of the door and head up toward the chain. She gave the door a mighty push, slamming it against the questing digits.

The fingers were immediately pulled away and the door shut with a satisfying click. She flipped the deadlock into place and smiled grimly when she heard the big man swearing through the wood. "Fuck, lass. Are ye tryin' to break me fingers?"

Ooh. This one had a Scottish accent. And apparently Leith's accent got thicker when he was in pain.

"The two of you need to get lost before I call the police," she called through the door.

"Och, we don't have time for this," Leith shouted.

Seconds later, the blond giant materialized in front of her.

Shrieking, Sunny stumbled back until she was flat against the wall. Why did she have to leave her phone all the way on the other side of the room?

Muttering under his breath, Leith flipped the dead-lock and slid the chain off, letting Matthew into the room.

The shorter man closed the door quickly and took a quick step toward her, holding his hands up as if to show her he wasn't going to hurt her. "Relax, Sunny. We're here to tell you about what's happening, that's all. If your parents had lived, you would have already known all about this. In fact, you would have been transported to the MacAlister castle at the first sign of your magic."

Were these people insane? "Magic? *Magic*? Don't come any closer," she warned when Leith took a few steps toward her.

Matthew reached out and made a beckoning motion to her. "We're not joking," he said. "We'll tell you everything you need to know once we're on the plane. But we should really get moving. It's not safe to stay here, especially now."

A hysterical giggle escaped her. "You think I'm going with you? Do I look stupid to you?"

Leith growled and made a slashing motion. "Lass, 'tis past time we left. Doona make this harder than it has to be."

It seemed irritation also made the Scot's accent thicker. Maybe it was best not to annoy the crazy men. "Look, if you leave, I won't call the police. We'll just forget this ever happened."

Leith laughed harshly. Reasoning with him was obviously not going to work.

Matthew patted the bigger man on the arm. "Relax,

Leith. Let's explain some of it to her immediately, okay? I would be freaked out too if I was in her position."

Shoving his hands through his long hair, causing some of the blond locks to escape the ponytail, Leith sighed and nodded. "Do it quickly, lad. I'm getting the twitchy sensation that says someone's on our tail."

"Okay, Sunny—can I call you Sunny?—it's pretty simple actually. You're a witch. A fire handler, actually. Anyway, there's only one handler for each element at a time. When a handler dies, another one is born sometime in the same year. They don't come into their powers until they turn twenty-five, which is why you haven't been able to summon or create fire until recently."

Sunny held up her hand. "You guys are wacko." Still, how did they know about the fires that had been happening since her twenty-fifth birthday?

"We weren't aware that your parents had a child," Leith said suddenly. "Had we been aware of you when we learned about their deaths, you would have been raised at MacAlister castle. When certain signs appeared as a child, you would have been watched very carefully. None of this would have been necessary."

Matthew nodded and looked over his shoulder toward the door. "The ADHD, the problems controlling your temper, the delusions and hallucinations you had as a child are all signs of a handler."

It was eerie, really, how accurate Matthew was about her childhood. Still, she wasn't impressed. "All it takes is one good hacker to break into my medical records to find out the same stuff."

"God's blood, child. Why would we break into your medical files if our intention was to simply hurt ya?"

Geez, this Leith guy was sounding older and older by the second. If she hadn't been so concerned for her life, she would have been fascinated. He stood there, looking all modern and sophisticated and then broke out in sayings like *God's blood*. It was almost as if he belonged in a different time.

"You're right," Matthew agreed, pulling her attention back to the situation at hand. "But what about lately? You've had the feeling like there's something growing in you, right? Like your skin will split if you don't release some of the buildup. And when you experience a strong emotion, fires tend to spring up. After the fires, you don't feel like you're going to explode for a little while, right?"

Sunny's jaw just about hit the ground. She definitely hadn't told anyone about those feelings.

" 'Tis your magic, lass. When ye were a wee girl, the magic had no way out, but it was muted somewhat. It would have manifested in physical symptoms, diagnosed as ADHD. Now ye've come into yer magic, and it's too big to contain. Ye need to release it, and if ye don' know how, it will find a way to release on its own. Ye need to be trained on how to use it properly, or ye'll keep having accidents."

"And you can train me?" she scoffed. "Look, I've always figured things out by myself. I'll figure this out myself too."

Matthew shook his head and pointed to the curtain. "Are you going to be able to figure out how to put the fire out before it burns down the motel?"

Sunny risked a glance in the direction Matthew pointed and gasped. Flames were licking up the cheap motel curtain, steadily crawling toward the ceiling. *Crap.* There wasn't even a fire extinguisher in the damn room and by the time she ran to the office to get one, the fire would be too big for the extinguisher to handle.

The two men stared at her as if they were waiting for

her to do something. "Well?" Leith said with a sneer. "Figure out how to call it back."

Call it back? What the hell was he talking about? Panic started to settle over her. Her heart began pounding against her sternum, and she panted as if she was running a marathon.

Immediately, the fire roared, shooting higher and spreading wider. It seemed to be responding to her reactions, and not in a good way.

"Leith," Matthew implored. He sounded nervous for the first time since he'd strolled into her room. "You can put it out, right?"

The bigger man frowned but nodded. "She doesn't have enough strength to prevent me from putting it out." He narrowed his eyes and muttered something under his breath.

The flames got smaller but didn't go out completely.

Leith growled and stared at the flames, his face the picture of extreme concentration. This time, the muttered words were accompanied by a waving motion. The fire went out reluctantly, if you could describe fire as reluctant. It certainly took its time dying out.

The bigger man waved his hands again and the room was instantly back to the way it was before she fried it. No damage to the curtains, no smoke stains, nothing to even suggest the place had been on fire just seconds ago.

Matthew wasn't staring around the room like Sunny. He was staring at Leith. "I've never seen you have trouble with anything before," he said.

"Well, I'm not able to control either Anna's or Sloan's magic. I could only manipulate Ms. Kerrigan's because she's so untrained, but she's very strong. Once her magic is firmly under her command, it will be impossible for anyone to stop her," Leith said, his accent fading a little now that the immediate danger had passed.

Sunny said the only thing that came to mind. "Holy shit."

Matthew scurried over to the window and peeked outside. "Leith, there's someone watching. I'm pretty sure he was there when we first came."

Oh man, apparently things could get worse. "There have been people following me for a couple of weeks. I thought it was just my imagination."

Was telling these two strangers about her stalkers really such a good idea? Then again, this whole situation was completely unbelievable.

Leith's eyes widened. "We have less time than I thought. Matthew, do you recognize the watcher as a Takahashi or Keita?"

Before Sunny could ask what a Takahashi or Keita was, Matthew backed away from the window with another slightly panicked look on his face. "No one I know. But Leith, he's wearing a turtleneck. In July."

Leith rubbed his palms over his face. "Hunter."

"What's a hunter?" Sunny asked, completely spooked by the petrified expression on Matthew's face.

This time, the knock on the door did more than annoy her. It scared the crap out of her. "Is everyone okay?" the red head in the sweater asked as he opened the door and poked his head in.

"Yes," Leith said shortly, attempting to push the door closed, but the stranger was already more than halfway in.

"But I saw smoke," the guy insisted, stepping inside and locking the door.

"You're mistaken," Matthew said, edging closer to Sunny.

Why the hell hadn't she locked the door after Leith and Matthew had entered? Oh yeah, they were crazy and she'd been trying to get away from them. Suddenly, Leith and Matthew didn't seem so bad.

Especially when the young man pulled out two guns, pointing one straight at Sunny's head and the other at Leith's chest. "I don't think so. Seems you found your new fire handler."

"Matthew," Leith barked as he lunged for the red head.

As if he was responding to a command, Matthew flew at Sunny, flattening her against the wall and tucking her head under his chin.

Matthew's body blocked her view but nothing muffled the noises. Fear flooded through her, nearly suffocating her. A shriek split the air and Sunny gripped Matthew's shirt. Her heart pounded even harder than it had before, and she actually wondered if she was about to pass out.

A low, soothing voice started muttering in her ear. "It's all right, Sunny. You're safe," Matthew crooned. Matthew sounded completely calm, which was entirely at odds with his previous demeanor.

Sunny pulled away and peeked around his shoulder. The hunter was on the ground, writhing in pain, both hands clutched to his chest. "What did you do to him?" she asked Leith, horrified.

"Nothing. You melted the guns."

Sunny looked at the twisted mess of metal on the floor and shuddered. It seemed this was more than she could handle on her own.

"Oh, stop whimpering like a wee lass and get off the floor," Leith said as he hauled the guy to his feet. "Ye're snotting down your face, lad."

The guy really was sobbing, tears streaming down his cheeks. Looking at him this way, Sunny could see the guy was maybe eighteen years old. When Leith pried his hands away from his chest, they were charred nearly beyond recognition.

Sunny gagged at the sight but managed to keep the chocolate bar in her stomach.

Leith said something in a strange language and the mangled hands started to heal. Soft, new skin replaced burned flesh and the kid looked up at the blond with a confused look. "Why would you fix my hands if you're going to kill me?"

The bigger man snorted and shook his head. "I'm not a monster, lad. There was a time when your people and mine worked together."

"It must have been a long time ago," the kid said, flexing his hands experimentally.

Sunny watched Leith's face carefully, surprised to see a flash of sadness pass over his rugged features. "Aye. A verra long time ago." The accent was back, thicker than ever.

"I'm almost sorry I have to report you to the head of the hunters," the kid said quietly.

"You won't," Matthew said from beside Sunny.

Leith said something else and a blank expression settled on the young man's face. Gently, Matthew led him to the door and sent him on his way.

"We won't have much time, Sunny," he said softly. "Leith erased the hunter's memory for the last couple of hours. He'll figure out something happened when he realizes he's missing some time. Not to mention the fact that seekers from the other clans will be searching for you as well. With the amount of power surges you've been causing, they have to know you're alive. They'll never stop looking for you."

She experienced a single moment of hesitation but the knowledge that she would be leaving the room alive with these men, as opposed to ending up on the coroner's metal table with a bullet in her brain, convinced her to take a chance.

Tossing her suitcase on the bed, she started emptying the closet and drawers, dumping the contents into the bag. "Do you have to call the airport or something?" She wanted to get out of here as fast as possible. Once she was safe from the immediate danger of stalkers with guns, she could figure out what to do about these two wackos.

"No need. We've a private plane at our disposal." Matthew said the words *private plane* as if it was the most normal phrase ever.

Chapter Five

Sunny tried to control her excitement as she settled down in the plush seat. She'd never been on a plane before, let alone a private plane. The last thing she wanted was for these two guys, who acted like riding around in a private plane was an everyday occurrence, to look at her like she was some kind of naïve little girl.

Matthew pulled out a sheaf of papers and started looking through them, glancing up every once in a while. "We'll be taking off soon. Is there anything you need right away?"

She shook her head. She was too busy trying not to stare around at the sumptuous surroundings to really care about anything else right then.

Leith was talking to the pilot, his voice so low, she couldn't hear what he was saying. Whatever it was, it didn't look he was saying particularly flattering things about her, if the nervous looks the pilot kept shooting her were any indication.

Not happy, Sunny stuck her tongue out at Leith's back, earning a laugh from Matthew. "He's a little intense, but he's a good guy." Matthew cocked his head and looked at Leith consideringly. "Okay, he's a good guy if he's on your side. If you get on his bad side, watch out."

Sighing, Sunny flopped back into her seat and crossed her arms over her chest. She was well aware she was pouting, but she figured she deserved it after the day she'd had. "I guess I got on his bad side when I wouldn't let him into my motel room."

Matthew grinned and shook his head. "No. He likes you, I can tell. He actually talks to you. Do you know how long I had to work with him to get even a few words out of him at a time? Besides, he probably would have called you an idiot if you'd opened the door to two complete strangers."

"Put away that lower lip, little girl," Leith said without even turning around.

Little girl? "Hey. I know I haven't exactly had the most mature attitude since you've come around, but give me a little credit. I'm twenty-five, not three."

The big man turned around and pinned her with a stare so intense, she squirmed in her seat. Wanting to make sure he knew she wasn't about to be pushed around, she stuck her chin out and met his gaze steadily. His eyes softened and he strode over to her, tucking a lock of hair behind her ear. "You remind me so much of my Elizabeth. You're going to be the death of me."

Stunned, Sunny simply sat there. What was with the sudden tenderness?

Before she could say anything, Leith walked away again and pulled the plane's phone off the wall. He waited a few moments until someone obviously picked up the other end. "Raven? Matthew and I are on our way back with the new fire handler. Have Anna and Sloan ready to train her right away. Her magic is too strong for either you or me to train her for very long."

He listened for a few minutes before hanging up the phone. He didn't turn around when he spoke again. "I'm going to the back office to get some work done. Try not to set the plane on fire, lass. Matthew, if you need anything, just shout."

He didn't wait for a reply, nor did he actually face them. He simply rushed to the back of the plane and shut himself away.

Wow. Weird. Sunny turned to Matthew, only to find the man staring at the closed door of the office with a sad look on his face. "What?" she asked. "Who's Elizabeth?"

Matthew cleared his throat a couple of times before looking at her. She could have sworn she saw the shimmer of tears filming over his blue eyes. "His daughter," he said huskily.

She had a sneaking suspicion she wouldn't be meeting this Elizabeth any time soon. "He doesn't look old enough to have a child," she said instead.

Matthew's mouth twisted in a wry smile. "He's the oldest witch in our clan. He once told me he was born in the same year Columbus set sail for the new world."

Sunny could only blink. "That would make him more than five hundred years old."

Nodding, Matthew cleared his throat again. "Yeah. Witches live for a really long time. We age slowly after our twenty-fifth birthday. Most of us live well past our nine hundredth birthday before we start to age again. Then, the process is relatively quick from there."

Sunny chewed on the information for a few minutes, until the engines on the plane started. Buckling her seatbelt, she turned again to Matthew. "What happened to his daughter?"

"Ah, picked up on that, did you? I don't really know what happened, but Leith's entire family was slaughtered three hundred years ago. He's never told anyone more than that. I suspect our clan leader, Raven, knows but I don't think anyone else does."

Sunny suddenly felt like crying over people she hadn't even met. At least she had no memories of her parents. Some would say not having those memories was horrible, but she felt like knowing them would have made the pain of their loss even more acute. What must Leith be going through right now, having experienced love and then having it ripped away from him?

Matthew sniffled a little and handed her a tissue. "It's sad, I know. But, if you remind him of his daughter, then you're definitely in his good books. You might find yourself with a new father figure, actually."

She leaned her head back against the seat as the plane started taxiing down the runway. It might be nice to have some sort of father figure in her life for once. She'd never had someone care for her like that.

She turned her head to speak to Matthew again but stopped when she saw he glanced behind them at the office door. Understanding suddenly dawned on her. "You like him, don't you?" she said softly.

Matthew smiled again, a slow, sad smile. "Probably more than I should," he admitted. "But it won't amount to anything. He's never been anything but friendly to me, and sometimes I wonder about that. Besides, even if he was into men, I'm far too young for him. He'd never see me as anything other than a kid."

Sunny frowned. Now that she knew witches aged slower, she had no idea how she would judge someone's age. Matthew seemed very mature though, so he was probably older than he looked. "How old are you? One hundred? One hundred and fifty?"

Laughing merrily, Matthew threw his head back and gasped for breath. "I'm only twenty-seven."

Oh. Well. That was sort of embarrassing. "Sorry," she mumbled.

"Don't worry about it," Matthew said, slinging an arm around her shoulders and giving her a little squeeze.

They were quiet until the flight attendant came around with drinks. Clearly, Matthew took this plane often because the attendant handed him a cup of coffee without even asking him what he wanted. The woman looked at Sunny expectantly. "Um, do you have some kind of cola available?" she asked.

"Not a good idea," Matthew said. "Caffeine tends to intensify the effects of your magic. Until you learn how to manipulate your power to your will, you might want to avoid it."

Nodding, Sunny pointed to a bottle of orange juice. "I'll have the juice, thanks."

The flight attendant looked relieved and poured her the juice. "Dinner will be served in a few hours. Just call for me if you need anything else."

Sunny turned to Matthew as she took a sip of juice. "Can I ask you some questions?"

Putting his papers in a briefcase, Matthew turned to her and smiled. He seemed happy to have something other than Leith to talk about. "Sure."

She fiddled with her glass for a few seconds while Matthew patiently waited for her to speak. "Can you tell me about my parents?"

Sighing, Matthew linked his fingers and stretched his arms over his head as if he was searching for the right words. "Twenty-five years ago, there was a very bloody battle between the three witch clans. It was the same battle we lost our previous fire handler in. We also lost our earth handler. Anyway, we took heavy casualties and Raven decided it would be best if the members of our clan scattered for a few decades. He was trying to make sure the whole clan wasn't together in case there was another massacre."

She could see the wisdom behind the leader's thinking. It would have made protecting them difficult but would also have made killing the entire clan harder for the enemy. She wasn't sure what it had to do with her parents though.

As if he could read her mind, Matthew continued with

his explanation. "Anyway, your parents relocated to Canada. For whatever reason, they never reported your birth to Raven. I suspect they were killed by members of another clan but can't confirm it. Obviously, whoever killed your parents didn't know they'd had you, since you would have been killed too. If Raven had known about your birth, he would have brought you to MacAlister castle and raised you himself instead of you being raised in foster homes."

Sunny always expected that when she found out what really happened to her parents, she would feel something. Anger, sadness, rage or even relief. Instead, she felt numb.

A little disturbed she didn't feel anything at all, Sunny shook her head and changed the subject. "Will I be able to do the cool healing thing once I learn to control my magic?"

Matthew shook his head. "Sorry, you'll probably be able to do basic spells, but your magic is pretty much contained to creating and manipulating fire. By the way, Leith's healing magic only works on people who aren't part of the MacAlister clan. Which sucks, but it is what it is."

Sunny pouted for a couple of seconds before she thought of another question. "So, if I'm the fire handler, and you're still missing the earth handler, it means you have a water handler?"

"Yes. The water handler's name is Sloan Shirer. And we have an air handler too, Anna Carrow."

"You said every witch knows when a handler comes into their magic. How?" Sunny was fascinated.

"There's a kind of shock that runs through a witch's body when there's a big surge of magic, I guess. The clan's seeker, that's Leith, can use the energy as sort of a homing beacon. The rest of the clans send out scouts to try to beat the seeker to the new handler," Matthew answered.

"So, I'll know when the earth handler comes into her powers?"

"Yes. And the handler might be a guy." Matthew rubbed the back of his neck and glanced out the window as if he was uncomfortable with something.

Sunny gulped, afraid Matthew was reliving some kind of painful event. "What does it feel like?"

Matthew rubbed his neck again and sighed. "I don't know. I was born without magic. That's why I became a lawyer."

No wonder Matthew suddenly looked so uncomfortable. She didn't know quite what to do to make him feel better.

Leith rushed over and leaned across Sunny to look Matthew in the face. "I came out of the office and saw you were distressed. Are you all right, son?"

Matthew rubbed the back of his neck for a third time. "Yeah. Thanks, Leith."

"Mmm. Okay. Do you have those papers ready for Raven?" Leith asked.

"I do."

"Good."

"Right." Matthew's voice was cheerful but Sunny could hear right through it.

They both watched the blond man collect his coffee and strut back to the office, once again shutting himself in.

Sunny gazed at Matthew, her heart breaking for him.

Matthew blinked once and focused on her again. He gestured to her cup and raised his own. "Cheers."

"Cheers." As she clinked her cup to Matthew's, Sunny couldn't help but wonder what there was to cheer over.

Chapter Six

The flight seemed to take forever and Sunny yawned. All the sleepless nights had caught up with her, and she was having trouble staying up.

There was only one problem.

Every time she started to drift off, Matthew, who was bent over his work next to her, would yelp at her to wake up, yelling about how she was about to blow up the plane. Apparently, the closer she got to the clan headquarters, the stronger her magic became, which resulted in small sparks flying from the tips of her fingers.

She started to rethink her decision about not having caffeine, but Matthew's horrified expression when she'd asked the flight attendant for a Red Bull convinced her not to risk it.

Leith's reaction was not much better. He kept rushing in, looking more and more worried each time.

Finally, it seemed Leith had had enough. "Sunny," he said with a thin, somewhat stressed smile. "Why don't you come to the back? There's a bed you can lie down on. I can help control your magic if we're in the same room, but I really can't work at these dreadful trays."

She wanted to say no, if only to show these men, who'd kidnapped her for all intents and purposes, she wasn't a pushover. The thought of a soft mattress and the idea that she could let go of some of her rigid control on her magic, however ineffective it had been so far, was too much to deny.

Dragging her tired body out of the chair, she shuffled down the hall a little, only to stop when she heard Leith talking again.

He wasn't speaking to her though. "Matthew," the blond giant said sternly. "Where are your glasses? You know you get headaches if you read without them. And you're all hunched over. Why don't you come in the back with us and work at the desk? There's more than enough space for both of us."

She heard Matthew agree, and both men asked the flight attendant for more coffee, just as she pushed open the door to the back room and froze in amazement. If she'd thought the plane was luxurious before, this room upped the ante.

The bed turned out to be a queen sized mattress with what looked like silk sheets and a sumptuous, blood-red bedspread.

The desk Leith had talked about was actually a long counter jutting out from one of the walls with enough space for three people to work at comfortably without bumping elbows. The work surface had indentations on it where papers could be placed so they didn't slide around if the plane hit turbulence. There were even recessed pen holders built into the desk.

The chairs that were lined up at the desk, including the one Leigh had obviously been sitting in and pushed back when he'd rushed to the front of the plane, were cushy and made of leather, clearly meant for the user's comfort.

On the other side of the room was a bathroom, just visible through a half opened door, complete with a shower stall.

A warm hand landed on her shoulder and urged her forward. "Lie down, lass," Leith said. "Just rest for a little while. Matthew and I will be here, and I'll help mute your magic until we land."

More than a little stunned, because honestly, how rich

were these people, Sunny allowed herself to be pushed gently down onto the mattress. Leith even drew the blankets up to her chin and smoothed back her hair as if she was a small child.

She lifted her head a few inches off the pillow, in time to see Matthew sit down at the desk and shuffle his papers around. "I didn't want to disturb you," he said to Leith.

"You shouldn't be so silly, lad," Leith replied. "We've worked together at this desk plenty of times."

Matthew muttered some response she couldn't quite make out, but she was much more interested in Leith at the moment. The way he talked fascinated her. One second, he sounded like an ancient Scottish warrior, and the next, he sounded like he'd lived all his life rocking the twenty-first century.

She supposed he'd gotten used to changing the way he spoke as language evolved. He probably only reverted back to the Old English with the exceedingly heavy brogue when he was stressed or in some highly emotional state.

Her fatigue was far too intense for her to dwell on his changing accent much, however, and she floated on the edge of consciousness, aware of the occasional muttering from the desk but not actually awake enough to add to their conversation.

Still, what she heard was fairly illuminating. And eventually interesting enough to wake her up when the talk turned to clan business.

She was about to join this MacAlister clan thing whether she wanted to or not, so she figured she had a right to know what was going on.

"What are you working on?" Leith asked after they'd been in the back room for about ten minutes.

"It's a contract for the new start-up company he's interested in investing in," Matthew replied.

Through half-closed eyes, Sunny saw Leith's head kick up. "He's never invested in something so risky before."

"Mmm, you're right," Matthew agreed. "It's about time he did. He's not investing everything he has, not even close. Besides, he has lots of time to recover if it goes belly up. He's only one hundred and fifty years old and the technology he's looking at investing in has proved to be pretty stable so far."

Leith picked up his coffee cup and took a sip. "That's true. Are the contracts to your liking?"

Matthew shrugged. "It's pretty standard. There are some things I'm going to insist be changed and other things I'm going to ask for which I don't think they'll give me."

"You're a shark," Leith said.

Matthew gestured to Leith's papers. "What about you? We've found Sunny, so you're free, right? Well, until Raven decides to send me somewhere. Then you get to play chaperon."

Sunny wondered if Matthew resented the need for someone to accompany him but she was far too interested in what they were discussing to interrupt. Besides, they seemed to have forgotten she was in the room. Or at least, they thought she was sleeping.

Leith put his cup down and pointed at his own papers. "Tracking the dragons."

"The dragons? I thought you told Raven you couldn't sense them?"

"I can't sense them or seek for them in the traditional way of a seeker. But I can make some deductions based on where they were last seen." The giant sounded amused.

Leith reached forward and unfurled a huge roll of paper. Sunny could tell he was using his pen to point out certain locations. "The last known whereabouts of the dragon queen was here," he jabbed at what Sunny supposed was a map.

"Prince Gareth was spotted ten years ago here," he pointed to another spot. "And the humans have been reporting sightings of winged creatures here, here and here, all within the last few years."

Matthew got up and stood next to him as Leith picked up his coffee cup again. "You know, all of these locations are within easy commuting distance to the cliffs here. Do you think they could be holed up there in dragon form?"

Sunny shifted around in the bed, trying to get a better view of what was going on. Neither of the men noticed her moving around but she wasn't surprised. The amount of sexual energy flickering between them made for better entertainment than the best romance novel. She wriggled around until she could clearly see what was going on.

Matthew leaned forward and pointed to the map. His arm brushed against Leith's on the way, causing the other man to spill his coffee down the front of his shirt.

"Oh, shit," Matthew exclaimed. He grabbed a couple of tissues and tried to mop the mess up. "I'm so sorry."

Leith cleared his throat and grabbed Matthew's hands. "It's all right, Matthew."

Matthew had frozen with both of his hands pressed flat against Leith's belly. Sunny could practically see the waves of heat rising from the two men and she had to keep her hand tucked under her cheek to stop from fanning herself.

Matthew stepped back and cleared his throat. "Sorry," he said again, lowering his eyes.

Leith tipped his chin up with two fingers. "Doona

worry about it," he said, his accent back, stronger than ever. "I'll borrow one of Raven's shirts."

The leader kept a stocked closet on a plane? She couldn't even imagine how much the clan used this plane if they needed to keep fresh clothes on board.

"Okay. I'll pay for the dry cleaning," Matthew mumbled.

Leith cleared his throat and started unbuttoning his shirt. "I said not to worry about it."

Narrowing her eyes, Sunny pretended to sleep as she watched Leith strip the shirt off.

The man was positively ripped. He was simply gorgeous.

Moving her head a fraction of an inch, she glanced at Matthew. The lawyer's gaze was fastened on the other man, and the slight bulge in the front of his pants hinted at his real thoughts. She wondered, for a second, if Matthew would question Leith about their interaction, but Leith turned around and Matthew's face fell into a mask of abject misery.

Wondering what had affected Matthew so much, Sunny turned her gaze back to Leith. Winding down the man's spine was an intricate tattoo spelling a woman's name in Old English letters.

She was supposed to be sleeping, so she couldn't ask about the name, but she guessed it was the man's dead wife.

She swallowed sympathetic tears, only able to guess at how Matthew felt. She felt a sudden need to get out of the bed and wrap her arms around the young man. There seemed to be a connection between her and Matthew and, for the first time in her life, she ached to foster that connection.

Chapter Seven

Good God, when Matthew had said they were going to MacAlister castle, she had pictured a mansion. But this was an honest to goodness castle with arrow slits, towers, and an outer wall with a moat. A moat that had to be crossed by a freaking drawbridge. "You could have warned me," she muttered to the two men at her side.

"What did you expect, lass? We told you it was a castle."

Leith had an amazing ability to state the obvious. Still, the man looked down at her with something akin to fondness on his face. She stuck her tongue out at him and turned back to the castle. She had to crane her neck all the way back to see the top of the closest tower. It looked positively medieval. "Please tell me there's indoor plumbing," she said.

This time, Leith laughed out loud. "Yes, Sunny. The castle has been completely updated over the years. We have indoor plumbing and electricity. We even have the Internet and cable."

"Be honest, Leith. We still heat the rooms with fireplaces though. Can you imagine the cost of heating this place with a furnace?" Matthew said reasonably.

He dragged his suitcase behind him with one hand, the other occupied with juggling his briefcase and a set of keys. "Do you think Raven will let me park my car in his garage tonight?" he asked.

"As long as you don't get too close to my Porsche," a tall man said from the doorway, where he was evidently waiting for them.

Matthew broke out into a genuine smile for the first time since they'd talked about him not having any magic. "Don't worry, old man. I won't get anywhere near your precious car."

Sunny laughed at their banter but couldn't help but notice that Leith had gotten suspiciously still and silent. "I'll be leaving," he said stiffly. "If you should find yourself in need of anything, have Matthew call me."

He marched off into the castle without a backward glance or even a good-bye.

Raven sighed and approached them, taking Sunny's bags from her and gesturing for Matthew and her to follow him inside. "I'm sorry, Matthew. Any time I say something to you, he gets a like that. Maybe you have hope after all?"

Sunny stumbled to a halt. Raven knew about Matthew's crush on Leith?

She scrambled to catch up with them as they stopped and Matthew shook his head. "No. I'm never going to be the one for him. I need to give up and move on."

Raven bumped him with his shoulder. "Do you want me to assign someone else to Leith?"

Matthew shook his head again, this time faster. "No. I can't give him up completely. We'll just be co-workers."

"I hate seeing you in pain," Raven said.

Sunny backed off, feeling like she was eavesdropping on a conversation she really shouldn't be hearing. But she was happy she was in a place which had a leader who cared about his people.

If she had to be here, that is. She hadn't forgotten about the part where she had essentially been kidnapped. Okay, so she'd technically come willingly, but only after someone else had tried to kill her.

It was hard to hold on to her anger for the two men

who'd brought her there though.

Maybe she was crazier than all those psychiatrists at the hospital thought.

She used the time to look over the grounds. God, it was beautiful. She wondered why it wasn't teeming with tourists.

"Sunny?" Matthew called. "Are you coming?"

She rejoined them, happy to see both men were acting normally again. Following them through the door, she stopped and gazed around in awe. If she thought the castle was amazing from the outside, the inside took the cake. It didn't look at all like a stone castle. There were shining wood floors, rich tapestries on the walls and dozens of portraits scattered around.

"Just leave your bags there, Ms. Kerrigan. I've been remiss in my introductions, I'm sorry. My name is Raven MacAlister, the leader of the MacAlister clan." He held out his hand.

Reaching forward, Sunny took his hand and jerked back when a small shock went zipping through her system. Raven's eyes widened and he shook his hand as if he'd been burned. "Leith wasn't kidding when he said you were strong. I'm very glad you decided to come and train with us."

Sunny couldn't help the laugh that bubbled up. "You mean I had a choice?"

Raven smiled sympathetically. "Well, no. But it seems Matthew and Leith were able to convince you rather quickly once they found you."

"Oh, it wasn't them. It was the maniac with the gun that convinced me. I figured Matthew and Leith were the lesser of the two evils, if you know what I mean?"

Raven's eyes narrowed. "Guy with a gun?"

"Hunter," Matthew said with a small smile. "But you should have seen her, Rave. She melted two guns without even batting an eyelash."

"Ah, yes. Leith did mention something about that," Raven said.

"Raven?" A woman's voice called from somewhere deeper in the castle. "Don't loiter in the foyer. Bring her inside."

"Of course," Raven said even as Matthew's smile grew larger. "Please, come this way."

The threesome made their way into what seemed to be some sort of library. A woman sitting in one of the overstuffed chairs jumped to her feet when they entered. "Oh, my dear, I've been waiting for you for so long."

The woman rushed to her and enveloped her in a warm hug. Instantly, everything in Sunny was pulled to this woman. She felt a leap in the pressure growing in her, but curiously, she felt like everything was in control.

"Oh," the woman said, pulling back and holding Sunny by the arms. "I'd forgotten how intense our connection would be. I'm Anna, by the way. Anna Carrow. I'm the air handler."

Sunny looked at her in wonder. She'd never felt this close to anyone before. The thought of losing this woman sent her into a panic. "Why do I feel like this?"

Anna patted her arm and let go of her, leading her to one of the chairs and urging her to sit down. "Our magic is complementary. Fire needs air to function. Similarly, changing the air's temperature gives it much more power. It's natural that we're drawn together."

A little more reassured that what she felt was normal, Sunny grinned and sat down. "It's good to know I match with somebody."

Anna smiled back and sat down next to her. "I'm so excited to have another woman here. It's been just me for so long." She glared at Raven, who reddened slightly and cleared his throat.

Patting her arm again, Anna turned back to her. "Dinner should be served soon. We should make sure to tell the cook what you like to eat so it can be included in our weekly menus. Tonight is roast beef, I believe."

Sunny placed her hand on her stomach and shook her head. She was far too overwhelmed to eat. "I'm not really hungry."

"You should eat," a deep voice said from behind her. "Letting yourself get hungry makes it harder to concentrate on controlling your magic."

Turning around, Sunny was met by the sight of the most beautiful man she'd ever seen. He was tall and lean with short black hair and eyes the color of milk chocolate. He was wearing a pair of blue jeans which showcased his thighs and a tight, black, short sleeved shirt.

Raven snorted and rose from the desk he'd been sitting at. "You really shouldn't talk about anyone else's eating habits, Sloan. You barely eat enough to survive as it is."

"Whatever. I take it this is our new fire handler?" the man said with a sneer.

Sunny was shocked. Why was he so cold? She stood and offered him her hand. "Apparently I am. I'm Sunny."

"Sloan, the water handler," he responded, taking her hand and shaking it.

Another zap of power rushed through her and she jerked back. Her response to his magic was completely different from her response to Anna's. What she had come to think of as her fire, pulled back and pushed forward at once, completely at odds with itself. It was a disconcerting feeling and one she wasn't exactly sure she liked. It was pleasurable and almost painful all at once. It almost felt like she was on the brink of a massive orgasm with no way to achieve the final push into ecstasy.

Something passed over Sloan's face, maybe surprise, before he stepped back and stared at her. "I'm going up to my room. I'll see everyone in the morning."

"What about dinner?" Raven asked with concern in his voice.

Sloan paused and flexed his hands. "Just have someone send something to my room. But don't send any coffee or chocolate up."

He left the room without another word and Sunny stared after him. Did he not want the coffee because he was having trouble controlling his magic? If so, what chance did she have for learning control if someone who was as experienced as Sloan seemed to have trouble managing his magic?

And what was with the attitude? What had she done to provoke his ire? "What's his problem?" Sunny asked.

"Well, if you think about how our magic is complementary and so we feel drawn together, it makes sense you and Sloan would be subconsciously pitted against each other. Fire and water and all that," Anna said with a warm smile.

Raven sighed and pushed one hand through his hair, causing it to stick up briefly before it settled back down into thick waves. "Don't worry about Sloan. He's been going through some stuff for the last little while. He wasn't always such a jerk. But he is right, as a handler, it is good practice to eat something whenever it's offered, even if it's something small."

Matthew smiled at her and slung an arm around her shoulders. "Come on, love. Sit next to me and I'll keep you entertained." He guided her out of the library and into a massive dining room.

The table was laden with platters of meat, tureens of

buttered peas, serving bowls full of roast potatoes, a gigantic platter of Yorkshire puddings and several boats of gravy. There was so much food for the four of them, Sunny wondered how much these people ate. Even if dinner was saved for or sent to Leith and Sloan, the amount of food was staggering.

Despite the formality of the way the meal was presented, it seemed the occupants of this castle were pretty informal. Everyone served themselves, asking politely for the salt or to pass the butter when needed.

Sunny took a small serving of everything, realizing that even though she was nervous, her stomach was actually quite empty. She stuck with water to drink, taking small sips as she observed the three other people at the table with her. Raven snapped his fingers and the candles in the middle of the table caught fire. Sunny jumped. "I thought I was the fire handler."

Anna smiled and patted her hand. "You are. All witches can control the elements somewhat. But the MacAlister handlers can do far more than just control the elements. We can manipulate our element to our liking."

Her confusion must have showed because Anna patted her hand again. "Don't worry. You'll understand what I mean when you start training."

Sunny gave her a tired nod and looked back down at her plate, focusing on the banter flowing around her.

Raven and Matthew were talking about some type of investment Raven seemed interested in making. Anna chimed in every once in a while but mostly stayed quiet. If it had been any other day, Sunny would have struck up a conversation with the other woman, but her day was starting to catch up with her and she was exhausted.

She was almost asleep in her dinner when Anna touched her shoulder gently. Sunny jumped, surprised to find she hadn't even heard the other woman get up from her seat. "Let me show you to your room," Anna suggested.

Nodding, Sunny dragged her tired butt out of the chair and followed Anna. She was so groggy, she was halfway up a set of stairs before she realized she had no idea how to get back.

Would it be too much to hope the castle would have those *Where am I?* maps posted on the hall walls somewhere?

"This is the handler wing," Anna said as they passed a closed door. The gentle, warm feeling emanating from the room told her it was Anna's. Did a handler's magic leech into their surroundings if they spent enough time there?

Anna continued speaking about how the rooms on this side were larger to accommodate for a handler's increased power but Sunny found the woman's voice too soothing to actually pay much attention.

"This is Sloan's suite," Anna said as they passed the next door. Sunny could have guessed that from the cool, aggressive power being pushed from the room.

The next suite was empty and Sunny guessed it was for the still missing earth handler. The room at the very end of the hall had to be hers.

Anna confirmed this when she pushed open the door and stepped aside so Sunny could walk inside first. Her luggage had been placed at the foot of an enormous bed. There was a chest of drawers against one wall, a large armoire on the wall across from the dresser and a third wall dominated by floor-to-ceiling windows. The room was decorated in shades of rust and red, which seemed to call to make the fire inside her burn brighter. It was beautiful. "I'll leave you to settle in and get some rest. There are fresh towels in the bathroom, which is right through that door."

Sunny nodded and said good-bye, still a little awed over the room she'd been assigned.

Her body still hummed from all the power and, despite the time that had passed since she'd first shaken Sloan's hand, her arousal hadn't dissipated. The feeling had only intensified as she passed Sloan's room. And despite how tired she was, there was no way she would be able to fall asleep with this much lust streaking through her veins. Maybe a nice shower would help take the edge off enough for her to sleep.

The bathroom was freaking gigantic, but she'd expected it to be, given the size of the room. She contemplated giving the soaker tub a try, which was big enough for two people, but in the end, decided she was too tired to lounge around for long.

Stripping off her clothes, she turned on the water, stepped under the hot spray and grabbed a bottle of shower gel. The water worked miracles on her tight muscles but the bubbles from the shower gel slid down her skin, and collected at the very top of her mound, yanking up her arousal by about ten levels.

She slid her finger between her legs and found the small ridge of her clit. It flexed and then strained out, demanding attention.

This was going to be quick and dirty.

She rubbed it quickly, closing her eyes and letting the image of Sloan float through her mind. In her mind, Sloan knelt at her feet, nuzzling his way down her stomach and taking her clit between his lips.

She came unexpectedly, Sloan's name slipping from her mouth on a long moan.

The orgasm may have been short, but it was strong and satisfying. She shivered, savoring the aftershocks of her climax.

As soon as she could feel her legs again, she dried off with a fluffy towel and collapsed, completely naked, on the bed. She managed to crawl under the covers before her exhaustion overtook her and she fell asleep.

Chapter Eight

Sloan pushed the food around his plate. He wasn't really hungry but lately, Raven had taken to monitoring how much he ate. It was supremely annoying, as he was seventy-five years old, but he could understand Raven's concern. Besides, Raven was just being a good leader.

Normally, he would have eaten with the others, if only to reassure Raven and Anna he was, at the very least, still alive. But tonight ... tonight he'd met the new fire handler.

He had been stunned by how attracted he'd been to her and even more flabbergasted when he'd taken her hand in his. The power that shot up his arm amazed him. It warmed him through and set him on edge all at once. He should have been prepared for the sensation. After all, every time he touched Anna, a similar phenomenon happened. He was so used to avoiding Anna's touch, he'd forgotten to brace himself.

The power hadn't necessarily been bad, but it had been different.

The feeling of her soft palm against his had sent him reeling far faster and further than her magic, though. He'd instantly wondered what her hand would feel like slipping down his bare chest and maybe sliding even further south. He'd gone from zero to sixty in less than ten seconds and his dick had leapt to life.

Matthew had sent him a knowing look, and he'd had to stop himself from dropping his hands to shield his crotch from view. He'd almost joined them, but he'd glanced up at the last second and looked at Dara's portrait smiling down at him.

Grief and guilt had swamped him, and he'd taken it out on Sunny before running for the sanctuary of his room. He'd hoped to spend the evening alone working through his thoughts but a knock on the door told him it wouldn't be the case. He sighed and pushed his plate away. "Come in."

Anna marched in and crossed her arms, sending him a disapproving look. "You should be ashamed of yourself, Sloan Shirer. Have you forgotten your manners, because I know you have them?"

Sloan was taken aback. Out of anyone, he thought Anna would have known how he felt. She had lost her husband in the same battle he'd lost Dara, and she would know how disconcerting it must feel to find oneself attracted to someone else. Then again, he'd have to tell her the truth about how he felt before she could sympathize with him.

He sighed and rolled his eyes. "You're right. I'll go apologize right now."

Anna smiled at him like he was a puppy who'd learned to pee outside and patted his head. "That's a good boy."

"You do realize I'm almost twenty-five years older than you, right?" he grumbled, good naturedly. He never was able to stay annoyed with the woman.

"I know," she said. "Now, go apologize and then eat your dinner. You're too skinny."

"Yes, Mom," he mumbled, edging past her to walk down the hall.

He heard Anna's door close as he knocked on Sunny's door. He waited for a few seconds before knocking again. "Sunny?" he called.

There was no answer. He briefly considered waiting until tomorrow to apologize, but he really didn't want her to go to sleep thinking he was *that* big of an ass.

He cracked the door open a little and poked his head in. "Sunny?"

The little redhead was nowhere to be seen. He hadn't had time to tune into her magic yet like he was to Anna's so he couldn't pinpoint her location. But where could she have gone? He stepped inside. He couldn't remember if this room had a balcony but if it did, she might be outside.

The sound of the water starting caught his attention and his head swung around. She was in the shower. Naked and wet.

Oh, good God, he'd never gotten hard so fast before. He couldn't help but picture what she would look like standing under the cascade of water. Her wet hair would be plastered around her shoulders and down her back, clinging to her body like wet silk. Her fair skin would glow and her small breasts would fit perfectly into his palms. Were her nipples pink or tan? Did she shave her pussy or was she natural?

Adjusting his dick in his pants so it wouldn't snap off, Sloan backed toward the door to leave. He was pretty sure being caught in Sunny's room would not win him any brownie points with anyone. And he was in enough hot water with Anna and Raven as it was.

He'd almost made it to the door when a soft moan caught his attention. His gaze snapped back to the bathroom door and he froze. He would bet every last bit of his magic that those were not moans of distress. His wife may have passed away twenty-five years ago, but he still remembered what a woman's pleasure sounded like.

Every drop of blood in his body drained into his dick and he actually had to press down on it to stop the orgasm poised at the tip. Shit, he needed to get out of there and fast. Tiptoeing awkwardly, he gripped the doorway just as another moan floated on the air. "Sloan..."

He managed to slip out of the room and close the door

almost silently before he sprinted down the hall. He burst through the door to his own room and slammed it hard behind him before unzipping his pants and plunging his hand inside.

Not even two steps into his room, and still fully dressed, Sloan gripped his cock with one hand, using the other to prop himself up against the wall. He set a fast pace, stroking his thumb over the top of his dick with each pass.

Sweat dripped off his forehead and onto the floor, mixing with the pre-come already pearling at the tip of his cock. The sound of his name from Sunny's lips was still echoing in his ears and he closed his eyes, a picture of a nude Sunny in the throes of orgasm forming on his closed lids.

"Fuck," he grunted as every muscle in his body contracted. The pleasure started at the base of his spine and spread rapidly through his entire body until he was sure he was going to pass out. He increased the pace of his stroking until his entire being was focused on the sensations between his legs.

He came violently, spurting all over his hand and clothes. He continued rubbing his dick until he was too sensitive to stand it anymore.

His legs were barely strong enough to support him as he stumbled over to his bed before sagging onto the mattress. He stared at the mess he'd made, another wave of confusion washing over him. Logically, he knew Dara wouldn't have wanted him to live the rest of his life alone. In fact, she'd probably be thrilled another woman had finally caught his attention. And in truth, it wasn't really guilt that made him so reluctant to get to know Sunny.

No, it wasn't guilt. It was fear. He had a feeling that falling for Sunny would be one of the easiest things he'd ever do. But as much as he sneered at Raven and the rest of them for believing in the prophecy about a war to end all wars, he'd seen the evidence of it himself. His magic seemed to be doubling in power every few days, almost as if in preparation for the coming war. All of it meant he could very well have finally found his soul mate. But then what had Dara been?

God, he was so confused. He'd loved Dara with all his heart. If she wasn't his soul mate, it meant someone else was. And according to the prophecy, he and his soul mate would be fighting side by side in the coming war.

An image of Sunny popped up, unbidden, in his mind's eye, but he pushed it away.

He'd already lost someone he'd loved dearly in the last war and it had nearly killed him. He wasn't sure if he could survive that again.

Chapter Nine

Sloan pressed his hand against his aching head and stumbled into the hall. He had hardly slept at all, and his sleepless night was starting to take its toll on him. He needed coffee to stop the pounding in his head. To top it all off, his body hummed with extra magic, and he desperately needed to release some of the buildup.

A door opened a little way up the hall. The only occupied room that far down the corridor was the new fire handler's.

Crap. Sunny was the last person he needed to see right now, especially when he was in such poor control of his magic.

He thought briefly about ducking back into his room but at that second, she looked right at him. "Good morning," she said brightly.

God, she was beautiful. Her full lips were tilted upward in a grin, and he instantly wondered what they would look like wrapped around his dick.

Shaking the thought from his head, he nodded at her. "Morning," he grunted, hoping she didn't notice the slight bulge his half hard dick was leaving in his pants.

Her smile widened as she stopped next to him. "Not much of a morning person?" she asked.

He cleared his throat and shook his head. "No. It usually takes at least a vat of coffee before Raven deems me fit for conversation."

"Mmm, coffee," Sunny crooned. "I love coffee. It's like liquid gold. But Matthew and Leith told me caffeine made it harder for me to control my magic."

"Yes, it can. But once you've learned to control your

power, you should be able to drink as much coffee as you want." Of course, he didn't tell her neither he nor Anna had had a drop of the stuff in weeks, as *their* magics were getting harder and harder to control. He didn't think Sunny would be particularly reassured by the fact that two seasoned handlers were losing their grip on their magic.

"Did you sleep well?" he asked.

Sunny nodded and stretched her arms over her head. He was pretty sure she had no idea her shirt had ridden up with her movement and a thin band of her creamy flesh was visible over the waistband of her pants. "I did, thanks," she said, dropping her arms. Much to Sloan's disappointment, the shirt settled back into place, hiding her skin from his eyes once again.

She continued talking, seeming completely oblivious to his gaze. "In fact, it was sort of weird. It was kind of like there was something dampening my power ... my magic, I guess. I felt like I could sleep without being afraid about setting the place on fire for the first time since my birthday."

"It's the wards Raven and Leith put on the castle a few years back. They're spells which help us control our powers," he explained when she looked confused.

"Does that mean we can't use magic in the castle at all?" she asked.

"No. A handler's magic is exceptionally stronger than anyone else's in the castle, with the exception of Raven. Even he wouldn't be able to stop you if you completely lost control. But as the leader, he does have a few advantages. He can lock down our magic if he wants."

She looked thoughtful. "So, he could take it away for a little while to give us a break from the sensation of needing to jump out of our skin?"

"Not really. He can lock it in our bodies. It doesn't

stop the magic from building up though."

She made a face. "Well, that's no fun." Then she smiled again. "But if I practice, the jittery feeling will go away, right?"

He nodded. "For a short time. It will build up again, but practicing will release it."

She started speaking, but he'd made the mistake of looking at her mouth again. It was full, pink, and a little moist from where her tongue kept peeking out to lick at her lips.

Sunny's smile had widened into an outright grin and Sloan blinked, finding himself completely blinded. She practically lit up the whole castle with her expression. Her name matched her personality exactly.

It was almost impossible not to move closer to her warmth, to her vitality, and something which had been dormant inside him for a quarter of a century stretched and reached for her light like a moth flying straight for a flame.

"Wow," she said. "You weren't kidding when you said you weren't a morning person. Are you okay?"

He blinked again, this time completely lost. "I'm sorry?"

She laughed and he could have sworn he heard bells. Had he ever been this taken with a woman so early?

"I asked if you would mind walking with me to the dining room. I swear, I need a GPS to find my way around this place."

"Sure. I was heading down to breakfast myself. And don't worry, you'll figure out your way around the castle soon enough."

Together they walked down the hall in companionable silence. She seemed happy to be there, which he found slightly odd. He would have thought having been forced to leave her home, especially given that she had pretty much been kidnapped, would have been traumatic. He'd expected her to rage against her situation, or at least be a little resentful. "How come you're not pissed about being here?" he blurted.

Sunny shrugged. "I can't really explain it. I've never really fit in before. I've always kind of felt restless, you know? I've always had these visions of fire I couldn't explain. I actually spent time in a psychiatric hospital when they couldn't figure out if I was a danger."

She fiddled with the hem of her shirt for a few seconds before looking up at him with a sheepish smile. "There's something about being here that makes me feel at peace. And something about the people here, especially Matthew, that soothes me."

Jealousy hit Sloan so hard, he nearly stumbled. She found Matthew soothing? What was it about the little pup she found so comforting?

Just as quickly, he pushed the thought aside. What did it matter to him if she found Matthew comforting? He had Dara's memory to keep him company. Except, it had been getting harder and harder to remember how she had felt in his arms. He had to look at her photograph now if he wanted to remember her smile.

He'd promised at their wedding to never love anyone else and it was an insult to her memory if he lusted after another woman.

Except he knew Dara wouldn't have wanted him to live out the rest of his very long life alone.

"Which way do we go from here?" Sunny asked suddenly.

He was really out of it this morning. They'd made it to the bottom of the stairs but he'd apparently stopped walking. "This way," he said, pointing to the left. The tone of his voice came out a little sharper than he'd intended, and she shot him a weird look.

He wasn't exactly sure how to apologize for his abrupt change of attitude, or if he even wanted to. All he knew was there were two empty chairs at the dining table and she headed straight for the one next to Matthew.

Which only left one chair vacant. And it happened to be right next to Sunny.

He sighed and headed for the table, knowing if he attempted to skip breakfast again, Raven would probably tie him to the chair and force feed him.

Matthew looked over at him when Sloan collapsed in his chair. "Having a rough morning?" he asked.

He resisted the urge to drop his face to his hands and grabbed a platter of bacon instead. How could he explain why his mood had gone from fantastic to shit in a matter of a few seconds?

"Apparently, it's a lack of coffee," Sunny said with a grin.

Why wasn't she upset with him? Hell, she didn't even look perturbed.

Nonplussed, he reached toward the middle of the table for the pitcher of orange juice. Sunny, who had reached out at the same time, closed her hand on the handle of the pitcher at the exact second his did.

The contact between them was electric. Literally. He vaguely remembered touching the end of a battery to his tongue once on a dare and the buzz and hum that had traveled through him. It felt like a line of cartoon sparks running up his arm. His dick stiffened in his pants and, amazingly, he realized he was only seconds away from coming.

Almost instantly, the sensation changed. It was as if his magic had become magnetized, and it immediately reached for Sunny's magic.

He yanked his hand back, knocking the jug over and causing the bright orange juice to spread across the pristine white tablecloth.

"What's the matter?" Raven asked sharply.

Sloan was about to say something sarcastic, or at least nasty, but one look at Sunny's face told him she'd been as affected by their accidental touch. There was no way he could play this off as his usual morning attitude. "Our magics reacted when our hands brushed against each other's," he said gruffly.

Raven nodded even as Sunny started rubbing her hand. "It's okay," the leader said to Sunny. "I've been told handler magic responds fairly strongly when it comes into contact with another handler's."

Sloan would have left it there but Sunny was already shaking her head. "I didn't feel like this when I touched Anna for the first time."

Raven raised his eyebrow and looked at them both. "Was it the same with you, Sloan?"

There was no point in lying. Everyone had seen his reaction. "Yes. It was a fair bit stronger than anything I've experienced with any other handler."

This time, Leith spoke to him. "Explain."

Sloan rolled his eyes at Leith's terse command but answered nonetheless. "My magic reached for hers with an intensity I've never felt before."

"Interesting," Leith said, tapping his finger against his lips. "I've never heard of that before. Normally, handler magic either repels another hander's power or feeds it. I've not run across a case where magics are reaching for each other, especially when those powers aren't being used."

"That wasn't exactly helpful," Sunny said bluntly. "You're something like one thousand years old. You should know something."

The silence which fell over the table was deafening. No one had ever dared to speak so frankly to Leith. Even Leith looked a little surprised.

"What?" Sunny said with a sheepish smile. "You were all thinking it."

Every gaze at the table was fastened to Leith, waiting to see what the blond giant would do. Instead of growling about showing him the respect he deserved, which Sloan had expected him to do, Leith burst out laughing. "You are so much like my daughter," he said when he finally stopped laughing. "Thank you for not treating me like an old man who can't handle a little humor once in a while."

Sunny's blinding smile was back in full force. "I figured you out as soon as we met," she admitted.

Leith's smile remained for the rest of breakfast, but Sloan was more focused on the affect the new handler had on him.

It terrified him.

As the morning meal came to an end, Raven cleared his throat. "Leith has informed me that Sunny's magic is quite strong and neither he nor I will be able to train her. So, I think it's best if Anna and Sloan train her right from the get go."

*Shit.*Sloan had forgotten the tiny detail about how he would be training Sunny. If his magic reacted this strongly to hers now, what would it be like when they were actually using their powers? Hell, what would it be like when they had to merge their magics? "Absolutely not," he said firmly.

"And why not?" Raven asked.

He said the first thing that came to him. "Because our magics are opposite. You know, fire and water. I'll only make things harder for her to control."

Raven narrowed his eyes suspiciously, and Sloan got

the idea the leader saw right through his excuse. "Fine," Raven said. "Stay out of her training for now. But when Sunny has enough control, you're going to have to work with her."

Sloan nodded, relieved he had a little time, at least, to work out how he felt.

In the meantime, all he had to do was find a way to completely avoid the new fire handler.

* * * *

Sunny sat, staring at Sloan, well aware her mouth hung slightly open. His excuse not to train her was complete and utter bullshit. There was no way their magics would repel each other, not when every fiber of her being was somehow yanking her toward him.

The man was returning to his jerky self, his true self he'd shown last night. She couldn't believe she'd masturbated to his image the evening before, much less had the orgasm of her life.

There was going to be no way she'd let Sloan know how much his refusal to train her bothered her. "It's okay," she said with another grin, hoping no one could tell it was fake. "Anna's probably a better teacher than Mr. Cranky Pants anyway."

She kept a pleasant expression plastered to her face until enough time had passed that she could escape to her room. Fake until you make it. That had been her motto for as long as she could remember. *Pretend to be happy with your life and maybe, just maybe, you can fool everyone.*

Faking it didn't help the pain though. It never did. And for some reason, Sloan's rejection hurt worse than anything else had in recent memory. Maybe it was because of the actual conversation they'd had on the way down to breakfast, when he hadn't been a dick. Or maybe it was the way her magic responded to him.

That had to be it. She had come to realize her magic

was almost like a living thing existing inside her. It wanted Sloan's magic badly, and it still roiled around in her veins, trying desperately to connect again with the man sitting next to her.

How could he leave her like this? It made her physically uncomfortable not to be touching him.

But he'd made his intentions to stay away from her more than clear.

She took a deep breath and hardened her heart against Sloan. Why would she set herself up for more heartache than she was already feeling?

Finally, she pushed her plate away and stood up. "When do you want to start, Anna?"

Anna gestured to her glass of juice. "As soon as I finish my drink, we can get started."

Sunny nodded. It would give her a little time to pull herself together. "I'm going to change into something more comfortable."

Without waiting for an answer, she hightailed it out of the dining room and found her way to the stairs. She bounded up them but stopped when she realized she had no idea how to get back to her room.

Cursing herself for not paying more attention when she'd gone downstairs, she peered up and down the hall, hoping that at least one way would look familiar. Of course, both ways looked the same.

Why had she thought living in a castle was a good thing?

"Lost?"

The voice was the last one she wanted to hear. Why couldn't it have been Matthew who found her?

"Can you show me the way back to my room, or are you too much of a jerk?" she snapped.

Sloan drew even with her and tilted his head. "Not so

sunny, Sunny? And to think, you had everyone thinking your personality matched your name."

She propped her hands on her hips and leveled a glare at him. She was so damn sick of hearing that joke. "Didn't you know? The sun can burn you too."

"Oh," said Sloan, motioning for her to follow him as he started down the hall. "So you're also a little fireball? Fitting."

"Listen here, you," she just about shouted. "What the hell is your problem? First thing this morning, you were all smiles, and now you're the most sarcastic bastard in Scotland."

"You know many men in Scotland?" he said.

Something about the way he said it, the possessive way he looked at her, made her grit her teeth.

Without even stopping to think about the consequence, Sunny raised her finger and poked him in the exact center of his chest.

Whatever she had been about to say flew out of her mind the second she touched him. Her power rose and seemed to latch on to Sloan. She couldn't have pulled her finger away, even if she wanted to. The feeling was entirely sexual and she desperately wanted Sloan to bend her over the nearest flat surface and slide into her.

It was Sloan who broke the contact when he stepped back and pushed her hand back to her side. There was no expression on his face at all. "Did you really not feel that?" she asked.

Sloan's mouth tipped up in a slight sneer, but she didn't miss the way his eyes focused on her face for a moment. "What I felt was similar to what I feel whenever I accidentally touch Anna, or another handler."

"Liar," she said. "At the table, you said it wasn't like anything you'd ever encountered before."

"It did feel like that at first," he admitted. "But the feeling has faded."

She didn't believe a word of what he said, but she didn't have a chance to accuse him of lying again. Anna came up behind them and squeezed in between them. She shook her head at Sloan and took Sunny by the elbow. "Come on, Sunny. I'll show you the way back to your room. Sloan? Don't you have some practicing to do?"

Sloan nodded curtly and turned on his heel, stalking away without another word.

Still irritated, Sunny stuck her tongue out at his back. She knew it was childish but at this point, she didn't care.

"Thanks," Sunny said to Anna.

"No problem. But he's not all bad. Before his wife, Dara, was killed, he was really fun to be around."

Against her will, her heart softened when she heard about Sloan's wife. How much pain must the man be in?

Not that it was any excuse to be a jerk, she told herself harshly. *Don't let your guard down. You'll only end up hurt.*

Chapter Ten

The water in the pond swirled as Sloan made it ripple lazily. He wasn't really trying to do too much with it right then. He was working off some of the magical pressure that built up in the last few days. Besides, if he did anything too drastic with it, he wouldn't be able to see Anna training Sunny.

It had been three weeks since Sunny had come to the castle. Three weeks since Sloan had first felt a buzz of sexual thrill awakening in his body after a quarter of a century.

He'd tried hard to avoid her at all costs. He'd been rude and mean. He'd stopped coming to meals until Raven had threatened to lock down his magic if he didn't eat. He had taken to isolating himself in his room— not very different from before. No, the only difference was that now, something in him desperately wanted to be out of the confines of the four walls and close to one person in particular.

Of course, he hadn't been able to avoid Sunny completely. Fate seemed to be working against him. He always seemed to open his suite door just as she passed by and he either had to walk down to breakfast with her or look like a fool.

All the accidental body contact didn't help. At least three times a day, he would find himself touching Sunny, whether their shoulders brushed against each other in the hall to reaching for the same platter at exactly the same moment.

If his magic was a separate entity, he would have thought it was angry with him. It had taken to zapping him every once in a while. And the tugging of his magic towards Sunny's was getting almost unbearable. He would have to figure out what to do but since it required he talk to Raven or Leith about his attraction to Sunny, he had yet to say anything.

And, God, he was like a horny teenager again. He had wet dreams at night, always featuring a very naked Sunny. He required multiple cold showers a day just to deal with the constant erections that seemed to spring up every time he encountered her.

He couldn't risk getting too close to the young woman, so he continued refusing to help with Sunny's training.

Raven hadn't been too pleased when Sloan had refused to work with them, but he hadn't had much choice in the matter once Sloan explained how his magic didn't respond well to Sunny's. The excuse wasn't exactly true. Of course, water and fire normally didn't mix well, but he was experienced enough to help Sunny learn to control her magic. He didn't want to get any closer to her than necessary.

Was it selfish? Sure. But he didn't know how to tell Raven the real reason behind his refusal to help train the new fire handler. The man had a never ending line of girlfriends and hadn't once found someone who kept his interest for longer than a few months. How could he possibly understand Sloan's fear of getting hurt again?

Still, it was impossible for him to stay completely away from Sunny. Her personality totally matched her name, and everyone had to smile when they were around her. Sloan felt happier just being in the same room as her.

Right then, Sunny was trying to summon a small ball of fire and manipulate its size. She'd managed to create the flame but it was either getting too big to hold or it was snuffing out entirely.

Anna instructed Sunny how to concentrate properly and, curious to know how the air handler controlled her own power, Sloan wandered to the other side of the pond so he was closer to the women.

"Calm down and clear your mind. Concentrate on the flames," Anna said. "Breathe from your diaphragm." She pressed her hand to Sunny's abdomen.

Sunny tried again but still wasn't successful. Sloan could read the frustration on her face and he ached to intervene. He had a feeling that even though air and fire magic matched well, each element would be controlled totally differently.

Over in the field, Anna spoke again and the brisk breeze carried her words clearly. Sloan wondered if she had created the breeze so he could hear her words. Was this her way of involving him in the training? "Once you've created the flames, concentrate on what you're trying to do with them. Like this."

Anna stilled and held out her hand. A tiny tornado formed instantly, dancing on her palm. "Now that I have the wind, I'm going to forget about creating it. Instead, I'm going to focus on the size and power."

The air handler was completely frozen even as the tornado grew in size. It hopped out of her palm and continued to grow until it was massive. She sent it off through the field toward the forest.

Sloan couldn't help but be awed by Anna's display. The tornado was huge, easily big enough to rip the castle apart stone by stone, and yet there was only a slight breeze. The air handler was manipulating the size of the tornado while keeping its power low.

Impressed, Sloan stopped playing with the water and watched the tornado's progress. Not even a stray leaf fell from the trees as it hit the woods.

Anna called it back, shrinking the funnel's size until it would fit inside a bottle. All of a sudden, it started ripping up the ground, chewing through it as if it had teeth. Once again, Anna had manipulated its size and strength, making the tiny funnel as destructive as a full-sized tornado.

After the little funnel had drilled a three-foot hole in the hard ground, Anna held out her hand and the tornado jumped back on to it, as harmless as a kitten, before making it disappear entirely.

Sloan grimaced as Sunny burst into applause. An unpleasant feeling churned in his stomach, and Sloan was man enough to admit it was jealousy. He wanted her to look at him with the same admiration. He briefly thought about lifting the entire contents of the pond into the air and fashioning it into a floating waterfall but then both women would probably figure out he was showing off.

Instead, he sent the pond into a series of waves, each high enough for a professional surfer to ride.

Glancing over his shoulder at the women again, he frowned to see Sunny wasn't paying to attention to him at all. Anna grinned at him, and sent him a knowing look. "Watch how Sloan can control the water in the pond," Anna said to Sunny.

Sloan tried hard not to puff up like a peacock when the redheaded fire handler turned around. He let more magic slip from him and the waves coalesced into one giant wall of water, big enough to sweep a house off its foundation. He let it hover at the edge of the pond for a second before sending it crashing down.

Instead of clapping for him, Sunny looked confused. "How does the pond have that much water? Is it really that deep?" she asked.

So much for impressing her. "I drew the water up

from the soil, too," he said. "If there had been an underground spring, I would have been able to make the wave much bigger."

Sunny nodded, a thoughtful expression on her face. "Can you create water?" she asked.

Sloan shook his head. "No, not the way you can create flame. Actually, I think you're the only one who can simply create your element. The rest of us use what we have on hand."

Anna nodded her agreement. "Yes. I don't create the wind so much as I manipulate the air currents to my liking."

"Hmm. So once you have the element shaped the way you want, you concentrate on manipulating it."

Anna nodded again, looking like a proud mother whose baby had just taken her first steps. "Exactly."

"So..." Sunny created a tiny flame in her palm and held it up for them to see. "If I stop concentrating so much on keeping the fire lit, I could better control it."

Sloan held his breath as Sunny narrowed her eyes and stared at the flame. It flared to life, growing and taking shape until it was the size of a dinner plate. Sloan backed away from the ball of fire as his face started to warm. "Try controlling the temperature," he suggested.

So much for not getting involved.

Sunny narrowed her eyes even more and he couldn't help but smile at the way her nose scrunched. She was far too cute for her own good. She let out a breath and the fire cooled. "Like this?"

"Exactly," Anna praised.

Cautiously, Sloan approached the fire. The temperature didn't rise as he moved and once he was close enough, he threw all caution to the wind. "I'm trusting you, Sunny," he said and stuck his hand in the fire.

The flame was pleasantly warm and tickled a little. It

was an amazing sensation and Sloan had to force himself to step back.

Sunny, on the other hand, looked completely panicked. "What the fuck did you do that for?"

Anna glared at him but patted Sunny on the shoulder. "We had to test it some time, dear."

Sunny sent him an angry look and Sloan retreated to the pond again, creating a whirlpool in the center just for something to do.

"The real advantage handlers have over other witches is that they can combine their magics to create something completely different," Anna lectured as Sunny began bouncing her fireball up and down. "Watch."

Anna summoned another tornado and made it collide into Sunny's fire. Instantly, the tornado became a fire funnel.

Sunny gasped and smiled. "That's so awesome."

Sloan stood by and watched. He could add his magic to Anna's to create a water funnel but it would only extinguish Sunny's flames if he joined in and the point of the whole exercise was to teach Sunny how to control her magic.

The fiery tornado rotated quickly, picking up speed and racing across the field. Anna frowned and twitched. "Pull back on your fire," she said to Sunny.

Nothing happened though and Sloan turned to see Sunny's face screwed up with concentration. Her normally milky skin was flushed and sweat trickled down her face. "I can't," she said in a strained voice.

"Concentrate," Anna instructed. "I'm going to dissipate the tornado."

The tornado disappeared but the tower of flames remained, dropping to the ground and roaring out of control. The flames spread out at a remarkable pace, speeding toward the castle on one end and the woods on the other.

Sloan pulled his gaze away from the fire and glanced at Sunny again. She was kneeling on the ground, panting with her hands outstretched. Still, the flames spread.

Understanding hit him at once. She had totally lost control of the fire.

The flames were bearing down on them and the heat was indescribable. No one would be able to survive if they were caught up in the fire.

Acting quickly, Sloan lifted the water from the pond and drained the surrounding soil of all its moisture and dumped the liquid on to the fire. The fire sizzled and died just short of the three of them.

Sloan stared at the empty pond and wilted grass around it. It would take some time before the ground would recover from him leeching it of all its moisture, never mind the damage it had received from Sunny's flames.

He'd never been so scared in his life. Not even during the last war when he'd witnessed his wife's death. His heart hammered so hard, he could barely hear Raven shouting from the castle or Leith's voice as he rushed over.

Turning, he came face to face with a dazed Sunny. Unable to deal with his panic, he took it out on the fire handler.

Chapter Eleven

Sunny gaped at the flaming funnel hopping along the ground. What had gone wrong? One second, she had been amazed at the fire tornado and the next, the magic had taken over. Sunny had tried everything she could think of to reclaim control of the flames. She had regulated her breathing, emptied her mind, and had stayed perfectly calm.

Until she realized the flames were racing for Anna and Sloan, and there was absolutely nothing she could do about it. Then the panic had descended and the fire had responded by gaining strength.

The scent of smoke still hung heavy in the air even though Sloan had put out the fire, and Sunny coughed, trying to clear her lungs. She stared at the ruined field, and started to pant. What would have happened if Sloan hadn't been there? The fire would have consumed everything in its path. Including the people she'd come to care so much about. A wave of dizziness hit her, and she locked her knees to stay upright.

"Sunny?" Someone was calling her name and she tried hard to focus on the voice, but everything seemed fuzzy.

A hand landed on her shoulder and she was turned gently. A face appeared directly in her line of vision and she blinked, still trying to bring herself back to the situation at hand. She only vaguely realized Leith was talking to her but the buzzing in her ears prevented her from actually understanding those words.

Her arm was suddenly gripped in a harsh grasp and spun her around. Sloan got right in her face and started shouting. "You little idiot. You could have destroyed the

castle. You need to get it together before you kill someone."

That snapped her out of her stupor. She blinked and
stared at Sloan. "Seriously?"

"Yes, seriously. Grow up, little girl, and control your
magic."

Out of the corner of her eye, she saw Leith make a
move toward them, but Raven held him back. Good. She
could handle this. If he wanted a fight, she'd give him one.
"I've only been training for three weeks. I wasn't prepared for how my magic would react to Anna's."

Sloan didn't look impressed. "She told you your magics feed off each other. What did you expect?"

That was it. A red haze covered her vision and her
hands shook. Small flames were shooting out of the tips
of her fingers, but she didn't even try to put them out.
"Shut up, Sloan. I'm doing my best. And it's not like
you've been bending over backwards to help me. If
you're so damn concerned, get off your high horse and
help me."

Something hot sparked in Sloan's eyes, and she had
half a second to take a deep breath before he slammed his
mouth down on hers.

They had been dancing around each other for weeks.
Small touches here, hot looks there. It had been driving
her crazy, and each time, her arousal spiraled higher and
higher. All the lust that had been building up in her, despite her best efforts to deny it, came roaring to the
surface.

Rage and passion fueled the kiss and she bit at his lip,
demanding entrance. He growled and opened his mouth
but didn't let her take control. Instead, he pushed his
tongue inside and explored her mouth roughly. She shivered when his hands cupped her hips, his fingers
tightening in a bruising hold as they fought for control of

the kiss.

Need rushed through her, pooling between her legs and making her clit plump up in excitement. She gripped a handful of his hair in both fists and pulled him closer so their teeth ground together.

They spun higher and higher, their breath mingling until they were literally breathing each other in with each inhale.

Her mind was totally consumed with one thing only. *More.*

Desperate for some kind of relief, Sunny pushed herself up to her toes and released her hold on Sloan's hair to wrap her arms around his neck. Once her grip was firm, she hooked one leg around his thigh and started grinding her pelvis against his muscular thigh. One of Sloan's hands slid from her hip to her ass and he kneaded it firmly while guiding her movements with the other.

A whimper worked its way up her throat as she rubbed herself quickly against his leg. This was it. She would have a spectacular orgasm right here, fully clothed and in front of three other people. But she was too far gone to care. She tore her mouth away from and buried her face in Sloan's neck.

A long groan split the air. "Fuuuuck. We can't do this here." Sloan picked her up, supporting her with both hands under her butt while she wound her legs around his waist.

She vaguely realized they were moving but it wasn't until Sloan pressed her into a mattress that she realized he'd carried her past Leith, Raven and Anna, into the castle and straight to her room. "Sloan?" she groaned.

"If you want to stop, tell me now." She shivered as he snaked his hand up her shirt. He skated his fingers long the bottom edge of her bra and started to press damp, open-mouthed kisses along the line of her jaw.

She should stop him. She should push him off and run as fast as she could. There was one problem with what she should do.

She didn't want to.

Throwing caution to the wind, she looped her arms around his neck and pulled him down. "Don't stop."

"Oh, thank God," he whispered.

The way he kissed took her breath away. He teased her mouth open with his tongue, licking his way inside and pulling back to nip sharply at her lower lip. "Let's get this off," he whispered against her lips as he tugged at her shirt. It went flying across the room, landing in a puddle on her dresser.

Her bra was next. When she was nude from the waist up, he kissed his way down her neck. His lips grazed the responsive patch of skin right where her shoulder met her neck. She couldn't help the moan, and Sloan obviously figured out he'd hit pay dirt. He sucked on the spot, nibbled it, licked it, until Sunny was nothing more than a writhing mess.

God, she was going crazy. She needed more, but Sloan seemed content to stay at the slow pace, slowly driving her mad. She whimpered when he pinched one of her nipples, rolling it between his fingers and pulling on it gently.

Threading her fingers through Sloan's hair, Sunny arched her neck and tried to pull him up for a kiss. He chuckled and settled himself more firmly between her legs. "Patience," he murmured before attacking her neck again.

What was he, a vampire? And he wanted her to show some patience?

Screw that. She hadn't been with anyone other than her battery operated boyfriend in more than a year. Her patience had run out as soon as he'd kissed her out in the field. She wrapped her legs around his waist and ground her pussy against his hard stomach. The seam of her jeans rubbed directly against her clit, and the sensation threw her over the edge.

Every muscle in her body seized and her whole world narrowed until it focused on the small, throbbing ridge of flesh between her legs.

It wasn't enough. Her sex was still contracting when she pushed on Sloan's shoulders and rolled him over. She yanked off her pants and underwear before attacking his shirt. "Too many clothes," she said.

"Yes, ma'am," he answered. He sat up enough to help her yank off his shirt and shuck his pants before he sprawled out on his back wearing nothing but a smile.

She pounced on him. It was her turn to make him desperate.

*

Sloan laid back, his arms raised over his head, and smiled at Sunny. He knew he probably looked a little bit smug, but come on. He'd made her come while she'd still had her fucking pants on. It had to be some kind of record. Even Dara hadn't been that responsive. The feeling was fan-fucking-tastic.

The only thing that could make this night better would be if he got some release too. And, if her fierce expression was anything to go by, he was in for the ride of his life. He couldn't wait.

Sunny, however, apparently didn't share his urgency. She straddled his thighs and took her sweet time staring at him. Instead of making him feel uncomfortable, the appreciation he saw in her expression made him want to preen. Soon enough, though, he squirmed with need. His cock stood tall and proud and he wanted nothing more than to bury himself in her sweet heat. "Sunny," he grunted.

The laugh that escaped her lips sent shivers of anticipation down his spine. "Don't worry," she whispered. "You'll get what you want. After I get what I want."

He shifted impatiently. "You already came. What else do you want? Because if it's another orgasm, trust me, I'd love to give you another one. Or three."

Sunny lightly placed her fingers at his collarbone and trailed them ever so softly down his chest, stopping at his nipples. She circled them in ever smaller circles. "Baby, I want you crazy for me. Now, hush and let me work."

"Trust me, I'm so hot for you right now, I'm about to combust."

She laughed again, low and rich. "Sloan, if you can still hold a conversation with me, you're nowhere near desperate enough."

He wasn't sure how much more desperate she wanted him, but as long as she was touching him, he was willing to endure anything. Besides, this could be fun. He stretched his arms out over his head, exposing his entire body for her.

"Well, that's a beautiful sight," she remarked. "Do you think you can stay like this the whole time?"

She seemed to seriously underestimate his stamina and will power. "Of course. Do your worst," he said with a smirk.

Raising an eyebrow, Sunny pursed her lips and looked at him consideringly. "That sounds like a challenge."

Man, he didn't remember ever having this much fun in bed. "If that's how you want to take it..." He let the sentence trail off, knowing she would understand he really was challenging her to test his self-control.

If he could classify a smile as being evil in a good way,

that's how he would describe the expression that crossed her face. He closed his eyes and waited for her first move.

Instead of saying anything further, she leaned forward and feathered her lips against his neck a couple of times. "Mmm," she crooned. "You smell divine. I bet you taste delicious."

He thought she would run her tongue along his skin, maybe kiss his ear a little. He jumped when she tweaked his nipple suddenly, pulling on it and rolling it between her fingers in almost the exact same way he had done to her earlier. An electric zap of sensation ran straight from his nipple to his cock and he felt a single bead of moisture run down his shaft.

Fuck. Maybe his self-control wasn't all that good after all.

Sunny didn't stop with playing with her fingers. She scooted down a little and took his other nipple in her mouth, teasing the nub with the tip of her tongue. Her teeth closed over it, almost roughly, and he couldn't help the shout that bubbled up from his chest. The pleasure was so intense, so sharp, he wondered if there was a nerve that connected his nipples directly to his dick.

How had he lived for seventy-five years and not known his nipples were a hot spot?

She spent a long time at his chest, kissing, nipping and tweaking his nipples. His balls had pulled up tight and he groaned, wondering if he could actually come from just that alone.

It didn't help when she settled herself on one of his thighs and draped her abdomen over him. He could have written it off as her attempts to get more comfortable, but her soft stomach rubbed against his dick and her wet pussy ground against his leg. Unable to stop, he tilted his hips a little so his cock pressed more firmly against her stomach.

He shuddered and thrust up again. His skin erupted into goose bumps and a bead of sweat dripped down his temple to land in his ear. The tickle in his ear merely added to the sensations rocketing through him. He kept up the motion of his hips, powerless to stop the steady stream of moans coming from his mouth. He was completely unable to control his body and the only important thing right now was reaching the orgasm poised at the tip of his dick.

Balls churning, he lurched up, only to nearly sob when the suction around his nipple and the sweet pressure of her belly on his shaft disappeared. "Sunny," he whispered, nearly frantic for something.

"Shh," she said. "I told you not to move."

He hadn't even realized he'd moved his arms until she pointed out the fact that he was gripping her shoulder. He forced himself to let go of her and reached up again. There was nothing solid for him to hang on to so he grabbed a pillow and balled it up in his fists, looking at her for approval.

She smiled and nodded. "You deserve a reward," she praised.

Oh, God, please let it be ... *yes*.

She sat up completely, held him with one hand and lowered herself onto him. He had to grit his teeth to stop himself from exploding as soon as the head of his dick breached her sex.

She was drenched and pulsing around him as she dropped down, taking him right to the root in a single push. "You feel so good," she moaned as she started riding him.

He couldn't answer her. He'd lost the ability to form coherent sentences as soon as she'd taken him in to her wet, silky pussy. He'd also lost control of his hands and they locked on her hips as if they had a mind of their own, helping her to find a rhythm they both liked.

She rode him with abandon and his eyes were rolled so far back in his head, he swore he could see the back of his skull. It was hard to pull his eyes forward again, but he didn't want to miss out on a single second of Sunny's expression. He just about swallowed his tongue when he finally focused on the woman riding him. Her head was flung back and she had cupped each breast. She massaged them, kneaded them, stopping every once in a while to play with her nipples.

His urgency went from about sixty to one hundred in half a second and he rocked her even faster, his orgasm just out of reach. His muscles tightened in preparation for the climax of his life.

Until she jerked away and lifted her pussy off his already twitching cock.

What the fuck was she doing? He whimpered, fucking whimpered. "Why?"

"No condom," she said roughly. "Do you have one?"

Shit, shit, *shit*. He shook his head. He hadn't had sex in a quarter of a century. Why would he have condoms lying around his room? "Don't you have some?" he asked hopefully.

She shook her head and bit her lip.

His entire body was sensitized with an agonizing need to come. He felt like crying. The cool air bathing his dick didn't do a single thing to quell his desire and he was pretty sure his nervous system had been fried somewhere along the way. Was it actually possible to die from blue balls? Because he was about to expire from lust.

Sunny pressed a warm, wet kiss against his chest again. "Don't worry," she whispered. "I have an idea."

What could she possibly have in mind that could beat

sex?

Before he could ask, she clambered off him completely and knelt between his legs. She cupped her breasts and bent at the waist until her belly rested on his thighs and his cock nestled in the valley between her breasts.

He groaned and thrust up. She wasn't large but she was soft and silky and felt like heaven. "God, I love your tits," he moaned.

Her answering laugh was low, seductive, and when she looked up at him and licked her lips, he lost it. "Sunny," he croaked. "I ... I'm..."

That was as much of a warning as he could force out before his orgasm hit him like a freight train. His eyes slammed shut and fireworks exploded on the inside of his eyelids. Every nerve in his body vibrated with the force of his climax and he briefly wondered if he would actually pass out from the intense pleasure zinging through his body.

When he finally managed to pry his eyes open, Sunny had sauntered out of her bathroom with a wash cloth. There were streaks of white between her breasts, dripping down her belly. Instead of wiping them off, she climbed back on to the bed and cleaned him up gently. When he was clean, she wiped herself down and collapsed beside him. "That was awesome," she said.

The matter of fact tone in her voice had him smiling. "Yes."

He cleared his throat, starting to feel a little awkward now that they had gotten to know each other in a biblical sense. He wasn't quite sure what she expected of him now. What he did know was he didn't want this to be a onetime experience. Deciding to go for broke, he turned to face her. "So ... should I go buy some condoms?"

His anxiety melted away when she grinned at him.

"Yep," she said. "And I would get them in bulk, if you know what I mean."

Chapter Twelve

Raven pushed his water glass out of the way and tried to focus on the contracts in front of him. Matthew had vetted them, negotiated the terms to better suit Raven's needs, and had okayed them. All he had to do was sign them.

But he couldn't get his mind to cooperate today.

Maybe it was the strong emotions he sensed flowing between Sunny and Sloan. Or Matthew's heartache over Leith. Or even Anna's uncharacteristic silence lately. But something was interfering with his concentration.

Whatever it was, it was clear they were getting closer and closer to the prophecy. He'd noticed that the handlers' powers were increasing by the day. Even his own powers, which had been established for years, were starting to increase. That had to count for something.

He swiveled his chair around and stared at the fireplace. He was tempted to start a fire just to stare at the flames, but since it was summer, it was really too hot. Instead, he stared at Leith's map of Scotland, which he had pinned to the wall above the fireplace. Black circles were around each of the locations where dragons had been spotted, or rumored to have been spotted. They were scattered all over the map and seemed completely random to him.

A red circle outlined the location Matthew had suggested they search. The suggestion had given him hope about finally finding their allies. He'd learned to trust his friend's instincts. The boy had never led him wrong. In fact, the way that boy's mind worked was a little scary. Matthew could never really explain why he came to the conclusions he did, but he was rarely wrong.

The cliffs. He supposed it wasn't totally crazy to think that dragons would hole up in a cliff. Leith had suggested it, too. It was just that Niya had always appreciated the finer things in life. Like indoor plumbing and electric heating.

He turned his chair around again and slid open one of his desk drawers. The framed photo was where he always left it and he picked it up, holding it so he gazed directly down at it. The picture had been taken in such a way that it looked like her eyes were following him. The colors were starting to fade a little so he whispered a spell to keep them bright. He had to chant the spell repeatedly these days. A twenty-five-year-old snapshot could only last so long, even when it was framed. He took it out of the frame several times a day, just to try and feel closer to her, which didn't help its condition.

He remembered her long black hair sliding across his chest as she straddled him. And her jade-green eyes would sparkle up at him as he licked his way down her body. The dragon queen had been spectacular in her human form and intriguing in her dragon form. She'd once taken him flying. It had been the single most exhilarating thing he'd ever experienced. Until she'd landed on a deserted tropical island, shifted back to a human and proceeded to blow his mind when she'd tied him up and had her way with him.

He traced the line of her jaw. "Niya," he whispered. "Where did you go?"

Raven stared at the photo, feeling his heart start to pound. He'd had a long and complicated relationship with the dragon queen. He wiped away the lone tear that had escaped. God, he'd been so in love with her. Hell, he was still in love with her, even after all these years. She'd even confessed her own love for him more than once. But loving the leader of an entirely different race was tricky. Especially when he was the leader of his own clan. Add in the growing tensions between the witch clans, and it'd been impossible to give their relationship the attention it deserved.

Another tear ran down his cheek and he took a deep breath, trying to get his emotions under control. He'd tried to talk her out of attending the training session he'd been running that fateful day. He'd begged her to stay home but she'd waved him off. It wasn't like they'd been expecting a bloody battle. All they'd been planning was a training session with the handlers. The four handlers had been trying to create a perfect storm. But creating a storm of that magnitude could be dangerous, and he hadn't wanted her anywhere near in case the handlers lost control.

Reluctantly, he'd agreed to allow her to tag along, and it had proved to be the worst decision he'd ever made. Niya had accompanied him, along with her son and her entire retinue of bodyguards.

The handlers had been successful in creating the storm but somehow, the other clans had heard about what they were trying to do. They'd found themselves surrounded by both the Takahashis and the Keitas as well as a large number of vampires and werewolf shifters. The battle had been bloody, with heavy casualties on all sides.

Somewhere along the line, the dragons had disappeared. He never found out what had happened. Niya would never have abandoned him, and it wasn't in a dragon's blood to retreat. He'd never figured out how the other clans had worked out where they'd be but it didn't matter anymore.

Raven still had nightmares about that day. He'd lost four clan members, including two handlers, people who he'd cared about immensely, and the love of his life all in the same day. And worse, they'd never told anyone of their love, so it wasn't like he could actually talk to anyone about how he felt.

For the last quarter of a century, he'd used all his free time searching for Niya, or anyone who could tell him what happened. But it seemed like the dragons had gone into hiding. He'd spotted Niya's son a few times, but he'd never been successful in getting close enough to speak with him.

Raven had taken to parading a constant stream of women in front of the clan. The women were actors, hired to act like one-night stands. He had used the excuse of going out on random dates to search for the love of his life.

Now, he wasn't just searching for Niya. The upcoming battle was growing nearer; he could feel it in his bones. And for the sake of his clan, he needed to get back in touch with his allies.

Leith had been snooping around, using all his seeker spells to try and figure out where the dragons had disappeared to. He'd searched the cliffs Matthew had pointed out and had yet to find anything. But the cliffs were huge and there were only so many hours of the day Leith could search. Raven would have joined him but he was determined to do right by his clan and supervise Sunny's training.

He stroked a single finger over the face in the photograph, cradled it to his chest and leaned back in his chair. He was so tired. He hadn't been sleeping well and it was starting to catch up with him. It wouldn't hurt to close his eyes for a few minutes.

A heavy knocking pounding against the window startled him and he nearly upended his chair. "What the fuck?" he swore.

He had to blink his eyes a couple of times when he saw the man standing at the window, beckoning for him to come outside.

The chair didn't stand a chance when he jolted up and took off at a run. He heard the clatter of it tipping over before he hit the hall at a dead sprint. He ignored Anna's gasp as he raced past her and out the door.

He veered right, his eyes searching for the man he'd seen at the window.

There.

Raven stumbled to a halt in front of the tall man and bent at the waist, resting his hands on his thighs as he tried to catch his breath. "Your Highness," he said between quick intakes of breath.

The prince crouched down and stuck his face under Raven's so he had no choice but to look the dragon in the eye. "Raven MacAlister. Tell me why you've increased your efforts to find us?"

Raven's heart nearly stopped when he gazed into those jade green eyes. Gareth was definitely his mother's son, and not just because of the color of his eyes. He apparently had the same habit of appearing right when Raven was least expecting it.

Raven finally caught his breath and forced himself up. How Prince Gareth looked so regal when he was dressed in a black T-shirt, even tighter jeans and bulky black boots, he'd never know. The man looked like he belonged on a college campus somewhere, but Raven knew the prince was probably hundreds, if not thousands, of years old.

Gareth stared at him expectantly, one eyebrow raised. "Well? I know you've been looking for my mother since the last battle but why has the search switched from her to dragons in general so suddenly?"

A soft wind blew around them and the scent of heather surrounded them. Raven closed his eyes at the memory the flower brought back. Gareth probably wouldn't want to know about how his mother and Raven had made love in blooming heather more than once.

Pulling himself back to the present, Raven looked at Gareth, careful not to meet his eyes. Despite the fact that Gareth stood before him as a man, Raven didn't forget he was looking at a dragon. And dragons were the consummate dominant predator.

"The prophecy..." He trailed off, wondering if Gareth remembered what he was talking about. The man had sat in on their meetings several times. But it had been more than twenty-five years since he had seen Gareth. It seemed like a long time to Raven, but to someone who was immortal, the twenty-five years had probably passed in a blink of an eye. So Gareth either remembered the conversations about the prophecy like it was yesterday or he'd forgotten about it in the hundreds, possibly thousands of years' worth of memories he had to sift through.

"Mmm," the dragon hummed. He cocked his head and his eyes shifted to his dragon ones momentarily. "You still believe that, do you?"

Apparently, the dragon prince remembered. "Our fire handler has been located. It won't be long before our earth handler comes into their magic."

Gareth shifted. "You're assuming the handler survived into adulthood. I understand you decided to scatter your clan after the last witch war. Why?"

Raven rubbed the back of his neck. "It seemed like a good idea at the time. If our clan members were scattered, it would be harder to kill us off. If we'd stayed here, we ran the risk of facing genocide. And with half of our handlers dead, our defenses would never have survived a large scale attack."

"I'm curious. Do you still think scattering your clan was a good idea?"

Grief tugged on him. His clan had been so much more than just the people he led. They had been his family, both literally and figuratively. In an effort to keep their whereabouts secret, he had contacted most of them only sporadically since they left and he missed them all dearly. "Yes. It was the right decision at the time. It has, of course, led to a weakening of clan bonds." He'd been completely unaware of Sunny's her birth. He wondered what else had happened to his people that he didn't know. How many were dead? How many had children?

"Mmm," the prince hummed again. "Interesting. But I fail to see why you've decided to search out the dragons instead of recalling your clan?"

"I'm calling on the alliance we made with your people. If we are to come out victorious in the upcoming battle, we will need the aid of the dragons."

Something flared in Gareth's eyes, and Raven felt like he was being assessed. "I'm not completely against the idea," the dragon prince said slowly. "But there will be two conditions."

Raven's head snapped up. He had not expected such an easy agreement. "Name them," he said.

The dragon prowled over to him, his eyes completely shifted. There was no hint of white around Gareth's iris at all and his pupils had elongated to look like small slits in dangerously glittering pools of jade. "You shouldn't be so quick to agree," the dragon advised.

"You are your mother's son," Raven said immediately. "You are an honorable man."

A thin stream of smoke drifted out of the dragon's nose, hinting that the beast was closer to the surface than Raven had originally imagined. He snorted and his skin flashed to the faintest shade of green, the scales shimmering in the sunlight before Gareth concealed them again. "I'm no man," he said in a low, growly voice. "I'm a dragon. But I am my mother's son."

Raven stared at Gareth's chin and stood straight. "Your Highness, your conditions?"

"We will not fight with a weakened people. The first condition is that you must recall your clan members. There is strength in numbers which you cannot replace with handlers, no matter how strong the handlers are."

Recalling his clan was no hardship. Some work would have to be done to the cottages on the clan property since no one had lived in them for a quarter of a century, of course, but he would love to have everyone home again. "Not a problem."

Gareth's eyebrows rose again. "Maybe not for you. But have you considered the feelings of your clan? Perhaps they have grown to like, or even love their new homes. And what of the children?"

Shit. He hadn't even stopped to consider what would happen if his clan didn't want to come back. "It will have to be something I deal with when and if it comes up. What's your next condition?"

Gareth looked at him consideringly. "Recall your clan. I must convene with the dragon elders before I tell you my next condition. I will be in touch."

The prince didn't say anything else. He simply turned and strutted toward the forest, transforming into a twelve-foot-long dragon almost instantly.

The beast took one long look at him and Raven wondered if he looked like a tasty snack to the giant lizard. A forked tongue flicked out of Gareth's mouth once before the beast took flight, apparently unconcerned about being spotted by humans.

Raven watched the dragon fly off, very confused but also hopeful.

Perhaps he'd be seeing the love of his life very soon.

Chapter Thirteen

"Sunny," Sloan groaned as she let the ball of fire fizzle out of existence. "You need to concentrate."

"I'm trying," she snapped, conjuring still another flame in the palm of her hand.

Sloan held his breath as Sunny started manipulating the size of the fire. He'd taken over her training after she'd nearly burned the castle down. Anna still helped out occasionally, but it was best if she stayed away while Sunny worked on learning control.

The fire dissipated and Sunny sighed. "This is hard," she whined.

Sloan fought to keep his lips from quirking up in a smile. She was so damn adorable; he wanted to throw her against the nearest tree and kiss the daylights out of her. "I know," he said, trying to soothe her. "It was hard for me to learn control too. And I remember Anna trying to learn. It took her forever. Don't worry, it will come."

Sunny pushed a lock of hair off her face and blew out a breath, clearly frustrated. "But it was easier when Anna was training me."

Sloan nodded and rubbed her back. "It was because her power was feeding yours. You didn't have to work as hard to keep your fire going. The air magic helped it."

Sunny plopped on to the ground in a heap. "Then I should continue to work with her."

Sitting down next to her, Sloan wrapped an arm around her shoulders. "You're doing great. Just think, everything you've achieved in the past week has been all on your own. There's been no help, intentional or not, from Anna. You've made huge strides."

"Thanks," she said tilting her head until it rested against his shoulder

She still sounded down, so he wracked his brain for something to cheer her up. "Have you been into town yet?" he asked, already knowing the answer.

"No. I haven't had enough time, really."

"Let's take a break then, and go into town."

Sunny agreed easily enough and before long, they were in his car, driving along with the windows down and the music blasting.

He couldn't help the smile that time, when she started singing along to the radio at the top of her lungs. She sang off key and her timing sucked, but she was having a ball. It was one of the things he admired most about Sunny. She really didn't care about what other people thought.

Parking on a side street, he raced around to open her door while she dug around in her small purse for sunglasses. Her smile of thanks was one of the most beautiful things he'd ever seen, and he offered his elbow reflexively.

She tucked her hand into his arm, and he reveled in the feeling. He let her lead him around, stopping whenever she wanted to look into a shop window, or coo over some brightly colored flowers. He stood still as she placed a silly hat on his head and waited while she took a picture of some children with their noses pressed against the toy shop's window.

Acting purely on instinct, Sloan bent down and plucked a daisy from a shop's garden. "Here," he said, offering her the flower.

"You shouldn't have picked that," she scolded even as she tucked it behind her ear. "But thank you. How does it look?"

"Beautiful," he said, well aware he referred to more than the flower.

"Ice cream," Sunny said suddenly, pointing behind him.

A little bemused by the sudden change in subject, Sloan turned around. Sure enough, there was an ice cream stand. "Do you want some?"

Sunny nodded and practically dragged him across the street. They got in line behind a small girl, who had hair the same vivid red as Sunny, and her mother.

Sunny crouched so she was at eye level with the little girl. "What kind are you getting?" she asked.

"Vanilla," the child said. "It's my favorite. What are you getting?"

Sloan watched the two chat about ice cream, stunned by the ease Sunny interacted with the little girl. Eventually, the little girl and her mother ordered their ice cream cones and Sunny said a cheerful good-bye to her new friend. "I'll have a chocolate cone please," she said to the clerk. She made to pull her wallet out of her purse, but Sloan put his hand on her wrist.

"Let me get it," he said. "What? Call me old fashioned," he defended when she raised an eyebrow at him.

Sunny sighed but let him pay for their treats. "Okay, but dinner is on me. And don't complain," she said when he opened his mouth.

He had to make Sunny see that all he wanted to do was take care of her. He might not be as old as Leith or Raven, but he was still from a different generation.

Still, he didn't say anything. He would make an excuse about going to the bathroom during dinner and then talk to the waitress about putting the meal on his credit card. He ordered his vanilla ice cream and waited patiently for the clerk to hand it over. A sudden sobbing from beside them drew his attention. Sunny's little friend had dropped her cone and was weeping as if her dog had just died.

"I know you're disappointed, love, but I only brought enough money for two ice creams. You can have mine," the girl's mother said.

"But I like vanilla," the little girl sobbed.

Sloan had never been able to take a child crying. He would do everything in his power to make her stop. And really, she sounded as if this was a tragedy.

He accepted the ice cream from the clerk and walked over to the mother and daughter. Kneeling next to the little girl, he looked at the mother and smiled. "She can have my cone. I've just bought it and I haven't even taken a lick yet."

The little girl's eyes lit up and she reached for the ice cream, but the mother shook her head. "No, we really couldn't."

He was about to protest when he remembered it was a different time than when he'd grown up. Parents needed to worry constantly about the motivations of strangers. He reached into his pocket with his free hand and pressed a note into the mother's hand. "I understand. Here, take this. It should be enough to get her another cone."

The woman tried to give him back the money but he refused. "A beautiful princess like this shouldn't spend such a nice afternoon crying."

The little girl beamed at him. "Thank you," she said, clasping her hands together under her chin.

He smiled and gave her a thumbs up. "My pleasure, princess. Now, make sure not to drop this one, okay?"

She agreed and skipped off with her mother to replace her ice cream after one last thank you.

Sunny's warm hand slid down his forearm before she linked her fingers through his. "That was nice," she whispered.

He hadn't done it to impress Sunny, but he saw no reason not to ask her for what he wanted, now that he had her buttered up. "Nice enough to let me pay for dinner tonight?"

She pursed her lips, which had him wishing he'd asked for something else instead. "No. But it's nice enough for a kiss," she answered.

"I'll take it," he said, leaning down. Very softly, he placed his lips against hers.

*

Sunny let her eyes close when Sloan's mouth settled on to hers. It was a rather chaste kiss, considering they were out in public, but it was still exciting.

She'd seen a completely different side of him today. He'd been patient with her since he'd taken over her training, even when she'd struggled to form a flame at will.

But that afternoon showed her something completely different.

She'd been pleasantly surprised to find Sloan was some kind of old fashioned romantic. He'd let her lead him around town, stopping obligingly every time she wanted to take a closer look at something. And while she might act like his insistence on paying for everything annoyed her, in truth, it was kind of nice that he wanted to provide for her. It hadn't really been anything she'd experienced before.

And then he had to go and offer his ice cream to a crying child, and then he paid for another cone when his offer had been refused.

Oh, she'd seen glimpses of this Sloan. He was a generous lover, always making sure she was satisfied before he finished. It was in the gentle way he now treated Anna, and it was in the way he spoke to Matthew.

It was enough to make her fall in love with him. In fact, she already knew she was knee deep in love with the man. All it would take would be a push and she would fall head first in love. And the little display she'd just witnessed had been quite the nudge toward that edge.

Sloan deepened the kiss a little, and she pulled away before things got carried away in the middle of the park. "You know what else it's nice enough for?" she asked.

He smiled. "What?"

"Dinner in bed."

"Yeah?" Sloan asked, sounding extremely interested. "Can I have you for dessert?"

Sunny blushed a little but tugged on his hand, pulling him in the direction of the car. "I wouldn't have it any other way."

Chapter Fourteen

Sloan dropped his head back and closed his eyes. The magic hummed through his veins, and it was slightly uncomfortable. His power had been increasing in spades since Sunny had come into her magic. Anna had said the same thing and according to Leith, Sunny was the only handler to have so much magic to control right off the bat.

While he still scoffed openly at the whole prophecy business, it was just for show. Why else would the handlers' magic keep increasing in power?

And the whole thing about the handlers having their soul mates at their sides during the war to end all wars ... well, he could see how it could be considered a sign.

Trying to pull his mind from his dark thoughts, he tuned into Raven and Leith's conversation. "Have you seen Matthew lately?" Raven asked.

Leith shook his head, but Sloan noticed the slight concern on the man's face. Everyone knew Matthew was desperately in love with Leith except Leith. "He's not been home at all then?" he asked.

Sloan leaned forward. "I saw him early this morning," he said to ease the man's worry. "He was on his way into the office." He didn't mention that the kid looked like he was about to fall over from exhaustion.

Leith frowned and ruffled his long hair. "The lad needs someone to take care of him."

Looking up, Sloan caught Raven's eye and shrugged. He wasn't sure if Leith was really that blind or if he just didn't want to acknowledge Matthew's one-sided love.

After all, the man did come from a time where homosexuality was condemned. Hell, in Leith's time, a man would have been killed over his sexuality.

Sighing, Raven sat up and changed the subject. "We really need to focus on convincing the dragons to train with us again."

"It's not like they made any difference the last time," Sloan grumbled.

Leith poured himself a glass of water and took a small sip. He was still frowning, and he stared into space when he finally answered. "Well, we weren't prepared for the battle. We were only doing some training, so the dragons signaled for reinforcements far too late."

A small breeze stirred Sloan's hair, and he glanced over his shoulder and grinned. Anna had summoned two tiny tornadoes and made them race across the table. It was quite the sight to see.

Sunny stood by the fireplace, forcing the flames into different shapes and sizes. She stared at the fire and smiled when it formed itself into the shape of a lightning bolt. "This is fun," she said.

Sloan couldn't help but stare at her. He'd taken over her training, and she already showed great improvement. Sunny was happy and it showed. She positively glowed, always had a ready smile and was nice to everyone.

Unless something pissed her off. Then she turned into a fiery little thing, like the sun itself.

He schooled his expression and stood up to wander over to the water feature Raven had installed a couple of weeks ago. Water ran down the tiled wall in a small stream to splash into the basin below. It provided a soothing sound, sure, but Raven had installed it for Sloan to practice on when he felt the need.

Looking at the water, he imagined it swirling. Instantly, a small whirlpool emerged. He amused himself for a few minutes by dropping things into the whirlpool and watching them get sucked down. Anything was fair game as long as it didn't disintegrate. Coins, pencils, and paper clips all made for good entertainment.

"Didn't you send a message to the dragons?" Sloan finally asked, pulling his eyes away from the water.

"I did," Raven said. "And I got a message back. I'm still trying to figure it out though."

Everyone in the room looked at Raven, and the leader started pacing the perimeter of the room. "It was from Prince Gareth." Raven explained the prince's conditions and how not everything had been finalized.

Anna released the tornadoes and they flew out the window Leith opened for her, dissipating as soon as they hit the fresh air. "I wonder what happened to the queen."

Sunny began swirling her finger through the air, drawing letters with fire and holding the trail in the air. "Why is everyone so concerned about the dragon queen? It's been twenty-five years since you saw them last, right? Maybe she got too old to make these kinds of decisions."

Anna blew at the letters and they all watched them float through the air lazily. Sunny's control over her magic had come along remarkably well for the most part. "Nice," Anna praised. "And dragons are immortal. So, if something has happened to the queen, we're all in big shit."

Sloan blinked when he heard the vulgar language slip from Anna's mouth. What she said was true, but he'd never heard her swear before.

"Anyway," Raven said, hiding his smile behind his hand, "I've agreed to meet Prince Gareth. He's going to send a driver once we've got the meeting date hammered down."

Sunny clapped her hands and the fire extinguished.

"Can I come? I really want to meet a dragon."

Sloan thought of Gareth. He remembered the dragon's human form as one all the women, including Dara, had fawned over. "Why would you want to meet an overgrown lizard?" he asked.

This time, it was Leith who shot him a knowing look. "You know dragons have human forms. He won't meet with Raven as a dragon."

"Yeah," Anna said dreamily. "And I remember Gareth's human form well. He's gorgeous."

Squealing, Sunny rushed up to Raven and clutched his arm, jumping up and down. "Now I really want to meet him. Please, please, *please*."

Jealousy made Sloan see in tunnel vision and it focused on an image of the little redhead and the tall dark-haired dragon prince in an embrace.

No way in hell would he stand by while his lover hooked up with lizard boy. He would be damned if he shared Sunny with anyone, let alone a Goddamned prince. Growling, he went all caveman and strode over to her and threw her over his shoulder. He stormed out of the room, hearing Leith and Raven's laughter in his ears underscored by Anna's outraged shout.

"Put me down," Sunny shrieked.

Sloan winced as she hit at his back with her fists. "Stop it, woman, or you'll bruise my kidneys."

"Oh, honey, I'll do more than bruise your kidneys if you don't put me down right now."

A shot of unease went down his spine, but he tried to keep his mind off the damage she could cause. Instead, he continued up the stairs.

At least she waited until they were at the top of the stairs before unleashing her anger. This time, instead of hitting him, she sent some of her fire down his back.

He yelped and just about dropped her, only barely

managing to lower her to the ground without dropping her on her head. "What the fuck?" he shouted, even though he knew exactly why she'd burned him.

"We might be sleeping together but I am not a toy you can haul around anywhere and anytime you choose," she said, poking him in the chest with a single finger.

"But, baby, I want you," he said, trying out his best puppy dog eyes for good measure.

Of course, she didn't back down. It wasn't who she was. "Then try being nice."

God, he was such a fool. "I'm sorry, Sunny. I really don't like the idea of you meeting with Lizard Boy, and I didn't know what else to do."

Sunny froze and looked up at him. "So you went all caveman on me because you don't want me to meet Prince Gareth?"

Embarrassed, Sloan pulled a Matthew and rubbed the back of his neck. "Umm..."

The smile on Sunny's face was pure siren. "Are you jealous?"

"No," he denied, but the tone of his voice wasn't convincing, even to himself.

Sunny sashayed toward him, her hips swinging enticingly with every step. She placed both her palms on his chest and slid them up and around his shoulders, tugging at him. He obeyed the gentle pressure, bending at the waist until his mouth was even with hers. "Don't treat me like a possession again," she whispered.

His need for her was so bad, his head spun. "I promise. What can I do to make it up to you?"

Sunny ran her tongue along his lower lip, and he promptly forgot how to breathe. "You can have your way with me in bed."

"Yeah?" he asked hopefully.

She closed the tiny distance between them and kissed the corner of his mouth. "Take me to bed."

Like that was a hardship. He cupped her hips and lifted her so he didn't have to get a kink in his neck when he kissed her. She wrapped her legs around his waist and grabbed the back of his head, pulling him more firmly into the kiss.

As much as he liked her taking the lead, he wanted—no, he needed—to take control. He had to show her that he was every bit as manly as a damn dragon prince.

Determined to take control, he licked at her lips, prodding them insistently until she opened her mouth. He pushed his tongue in, stroking the roof of her mouth and bossing her tongue around with his.

He stumbled down the hall, knocking into the ridiculous little tables Anna had insisted be scattered throughout the castle. One may have toppled over and something may have shattered when it hit the floor, but he didn't stop to check. Not when Sunny kept releasing those tiny little moans into his mouth.

He swallowed the sounds she fed him and was determined to draw more from her. Finally, he stopped in front of her room and he let go of her with one hand to manipulate the doorknob. He wrestled with it for a few seconds, trying to open it without taking his mouth from Sunny's.

Sloan growled with frustration when the fucking thing wouldn't cooperate with him. He was forced to pull his lips off Sunny's and actually watch what he was doing. Sunny didn't help matters when she started to mouth her way down his neck a little. Finally, Sloan managed to open the door.

He shuffled inside, kicking the door shut with his foot, and made his way to the bed. He all but dropped her on the mattress, and she landed with a soft thud.

She looked up at him, her eyes sparkling with heat and desire. It was all he could do not to rip off her clothes and sink into her. But he wanted more than that. She *deserved* more than that. "Stand up."

She bit her lip and looked up at him from under her thick veil of eyelashes. He almost forgot his whole plan with that one look, but he stood firm. "I said, stand up."

The bedding rustled as she rose gracefully from the mattress. She glided to the center of the room and froze. "Now what?" Her voice was sultry and drove his lust even higher. The expression on her face was one of pure desire. Clearly, she liked it when he got a little dominating. "Strip."

If there was any doubt she would disobey his order, it was quickly dispelled when she grabbed the hem of her shirt and pulled it over her head. The movement was slow, revealing one creamy inch of skin at a time, and his already hard dick twitched, eager to get inside her.

His mouth practically watered by the time he removed his shirt. Sunny's mouth formed into a tiny, Mona Lisa smile as she swept her hair over her shoulder and reached behind her back to unhook her bra. "Stop," he growled.

She froze, her hands still behind her back. Sloan had been dreaming of one particular scene since their first encounter, and it was time to make his dream come true. "The pants first."

Sunny obeyed him easily, moving her hands from her bra to the front of her jeans and popping open the button without hesitation. She peeled the denim from her slim legs and tossed the pants over her shoulder. A tiny scrap of blue silk covered her pussy from his gaze, matching the blue bra that cupped her perfect breasts lovingly.

He had to see the entire sight. He stalked over to her

slowly, circling her, viewing her from every angle. He just about choked when he saw the tiny string of her thong disappearing between her creamy cheeks. God, she was beautiful. No, beautiful was too tame a word for Sunny. She was breathtaking.

His hands itched to touch, to stroke, but he restrained himself. "Bra next."

She complied. The filmy material seemed to float away from her body, leaving her completely bare from the waist up. "Have I told you how much I love your tits?" he asked softly.

Her arm drifted up her belly and hovered under her breasts as if she wanted to cover herself. "You may have mentioned it a time or two," she whispered.

He took his time, making sure he memorized every inch of her spectacular body. They hadn't spoken about commitment, and he was acutely aware that each time he made love to Sunny could potentially be the last. "I think this thong was created to give me a heart attack."

"Well then, I guess I should get rid of it." Hooking her fingers through the thin bands of material on each hip, she slowly slid the underwear down until she could kick it off.

She stood before him proudly, her shoulders straight and her head held high. Her red hair tumbled in wild waves around her shoulders and she looked like some kind of princess of old. He pried his tongue from the roof of his mouth and reminded himself that he was supposed to be making her understand why he was the better choice over some fire-breathing lizard. And right then, she looked far too smug. It was time for him to take back control.

"Get on the bed."

Once again, she obeyed his commands, even though her expression still reflected her knowledge that she had robbed him of all sense. Clambering up onto the mattress, Sunny sprawled on her back, legs open slightly so he could see the folds of her pussy. "Like this?"

His entire body throbbed in anticipation, and he knew he would never make it through this, would never succeed with his mission, if she touched him. Thinking quickly, he slid off his belt, wrapped it around her wrists, and secured her to the headboard. "Oh, kinky," she breathed.

"You haven't seen anything yet." He looked around the room, hoping he could find something, anything, he could use to make good on his threat. His gaze landed on the strand of pearls laying on her dresser. Her eyes widened when he slipped the necklace into his pocket but she didn't say a word.

He yanked off his T-shirt before joining her on the bed. "Aren't you going to take off your pants?" she asked.

"Don't worry about me." He skimmed a hand along her jaw and down her throat, pausing to tickle one finger against the pounding pulse point in her neck. "It's hotter this way, don't you think?" He certainly wasn't going to tell her that he wouldn't last if he stripped completely.

She shook her head and he pinched her nipple a little roughly in retaliation. She squawked, her earlier urgency obviously tamed by the time it'd taken for her to strip and be restrained. He wasn't disappointed though. It meant he had more of an opportunity to touch her.

He leaned down and caught her lips in a kiss. Then another. Then another. By the time he surfaced to let her catch her breath, her eyes were glazed over again. He pressed kisses down her neck and along her body, stopping to pay homage to her peaked nipples. He nibbled on them, licked them, and sucked them, until she writhed beneath him. Then and only then, did he move on.

He stabbed his tongue into her belly button, pleased by the little desperate moans she started making. He licked a trail down her belly to the very top of her pussy, where he nuzzled his nose into her sparse curls. He had never understood some men's fascination with the bald pussy. He loved Sonny's soft curls. They simply reminded him he was sleeping with a real woman.

Slithering down the bed, Sloan made his way between Sonny's legs and wedged them open with his shoulders. Using his fingers, he parted her folds and stared down at her. She was stunning, simply stunning. Her clit was swollen, peeping out from under the hood. With one finger he lightly flicked over the small ridge of flesh, teasing and coaxing the small bundle of nerves out from its hiding place. The little organ stood proudly for him. He fancied it begged for his touch. "Tell me, Sunny. Where is it most sensitive?"

He tore his eyes away from her sex and looked up at her when she failed to answer. Her bottom lip was caught between her teeth and her eyes were squeezed shut. He smiled triumphantly. This was exactly how he wanted her. "Your answer, Sunny," he demanded. "And look at me when you talk."

The expression in her eyes when she finally opened them made him want to pound his chest in victory. There was no way she was thinking about the dragon prince now.

"The right side."

The right side? Oh. She'd answered his question. Placing the very tip of his index finger on the right side of her clit he pressed down a little. "Here?"

Her answering whimper was all he needed to hear.

Her hips jerked when he wiggled his finger against that spot. "Please," she whimpered.

"Please what?" He knew exactly what she wanted. He

wanted to hear her say it.

She thrashed her head from side to side, her hair spilling in glorious abundance over her pillow. "I need to come. Please, make me come."

Her honesty deserved a reward. Sloan stroked her clit one last time before pulling his hand away. "Good girl." Closing his mouth over the small nubbin of flesh, he stiffened the tip of his tongue and used it to flick against the spot she'd indicated earlier.

She went wild, chanting his name and jerking her hips against his mouth. But he wasn't going to let her get off that easily.

Reaching into his pocket, he retrieved the strand of pearls. Making sure to keep her distracted with his mouth, he fed the pearls into her sopping pussy, one by one. When all but the very end of the necklace was in, he lifted his mouth off her and sat back. He pulled the strand up and over so each individual pearl bumped against her clitoris as he removed the necklace. "Who is making love to you?"

"You, Sloan."

He drew another pearl from her pussy and dropped a kiss against her soft belly. "Who do you want?"

Sunny sobbed and writhed. "You, Sloan. Only you."

A savage possessiveness flooded through him. He needed to claim her, to make her his, and to do that he needed to give her an orgasm so spectacular, she would never forget it.

He slipped one finger in alongside her pearls and pressed the beads firmly against the top of her pussy. He continued pulling at the necklace, making sure the strand was taut, so her clit was stimulated by each and every pearl. She was beyond words, and every muscle in her body was stiff. She was close, he could tell. If she didn't come soon, she probably wouldn't. Gathering together the small molecules of moisture in the air, he created a small jet of water and directed it to pummel against the right side of her clit.

She screamed, her body going rigid. Her pussy went hot and liquid around his finger a mere second before her inner walls began contracting on him.

Pushed past his limits, Sloan reared up and yanked his pants and underwear off in a single movement. He paused for one second to grab the condom he'd taken to carrying around in his pocket before chucking his pants on the floor. He sheathed himself, pulled the rest of the pearls out of her pussy, and thrust inside her still clenching sex. He could feel her heat even through the latex and it was enough to make him see stars. He hammered into her, unable to slow down.

Sunny's cries increased and she raised her head to bite his shoulder. The small pain merely spurred him on. "Faster," she cried when she released his flesh from between her teeth.

Faster was something he could definitely do. He increased his pace, until he panted like a racehorse, his lungs burning for the need for oxygen. Still, he didn't slow down until her eyes snapped open and stared at him with wonder. Her mouth opened in a silent scream and she convulsed around him, milking the orgasm out of him just like that.

He spilled into the condom in an unexpected orgasm, shouting her name. The climax seemed to last forever. He had just enough sense to roll to Sunny's side before collapsing.

He lay there, stunned. Never had sex been so intense. It was only when Sunny gave a small whimper that he managed to lift his head. Shit. He'd forgotten she was still restrained to the headboard.

Forcing himself to his knees, Sloan reached up with shaking arms and released the belt holding her wrists. In hindsight, his belt probably hadn't been the best thing to use as a restraint. The skin around each wrist was red and her hands were cold. He rubbed them in his own trying to warm them up and restore circulation. "I'm so sorry. Do they hurt very much?"

She shook her head and smiled. "Don't worry. They only hurt a little, and it was totally worth it."

When her hands were finally warm Sloan hopped off the bed and quickly took care of the condom. "Do you need anything?"

Sunny bit her lip, looking hesitant for the first time. "Would you mind holding me for a little while?"

He rejoined her on the bed and pulled her into his arms. She nestled against him, burying her nose in the hollow of his throat. "You don't even have to ask," he whispered.

Chapter Fifteen

A shaft of light hit him straight in the face and Sloan groaned a little. He already knew he wasn't in his own room. The scent of wild flowers was a dead giveaway. Opening his eyes, Sloan stared at the woman next to him. Her red hair was spread out over the pillow, and her fist was curled up loosely by her face. She looked positively angelic, even though he knew she could be a little hellion when she put her mind to it.

Sunny shifted around, moving closer and closer, until she was snuggled right up against him. She nuzzled her nose against his shoulder and wrapped herself around his arm before throwing her leg over his thigh.

A smile broke over his face. He was pleasantly surprised at how much he actually liked the cuddling. He'd never actually nestled up with a woman before. Dara had always liked her space in bed and he'd never complained.

An ache formed in his chest, and he rubbed at it. He recognized the sweet pain. It was love, pure and simple. He should have guessed his feelings for Sunny had developed past the grudging admiration he'd first felt and into something much more when jealousy had overwhelmed him at the thought of her meeting the dragon prince.

For the first time in a long time, Sloan didn't feel a crushing agony when he thought about Dara. He knew what he needed to do. It was time for him to let go.

Easing out of Sunny's hold, Sloan slid from the bed and slipped on his pants. He tiptoed into the hall, closing the door softly behind him. It was early enough that he didn't need to worry about being caught leaving the fire handler's room. Not that anyone was clueless about their relationship. Every single occupant of the castle had teased him about it at least once since he started seeing Sunny.

Still, he didn't know what Sunny would think if anyone caught him sneaking out of her room, so he hauled ass down the hall to his own suite.

He looked around the bedroom and sank onto the bed. This room hadn't changed in more than twenty-five years. Stroking the blue bedspread, Sloan thought back to the day he'd walked in and found his suite totally redone. Dara had giggled and asked if he'd loved it. He'd loved it because she had done it for him.

This room didn't seem like his anymore. In fact, he hadn't done more than shower and change clothes in his room in weeks. His mind set on what he knew he had to do, he dressed quickly and took a deep breath.

Dara's picture smiled up at him from his dresser, right next to the vase that held her ashes. He picked up the photo and looked at it, tracing his finger over the line of her jaw. "Dara, sweetie..." He stopped to clear his throat as tears misted over his vision. "I love you. You'll always be the first woman I ever loved."

He took a deep breath and continued speaking to the picture as if he was really talking to his dead wife. "But I'm in love with Sunny. I hope that's okay."

Sloan knew in his heart Dara wouldn't want him to live alone and miserable for the rest of his very long life. And talking to Dara like this felt good. "You'd really like her. She's a feisty one, that's for sure. And don't worry. She won't let me get away with any shit."

Resolved, he placed the photo on his bed. It was time to really let her go. He wasn't doing her memory any justice be refusing to move on. He picked up the urn containing her ashes and carried it outside. Sitting down on the dew-dampened grass, he held the vase against his heart for a moment. It would be the last time he held her close and he wanted to take a few more seconds to really cherish her.

"Can I sit?"

Sloan jumped when Anna lowered herself to the ground without waiting for an answer. He hadn't even heard her approach him. "What are you doing out here so early?" he asked, shifting around so he could see her clearly.

She shrugged and pulled her legs close to her chest, resting her chin on her knees. "Addison brought me here once to see the sun rise. I come here all the time now. I try to remember his smile and how he smelled and how his arms felt around me."

Guilt swamped him. Had he really been so oblivious all these years? "I'm sorry," he whispered, draping an arm across her shoulders. "Sometimes I forget I'm not the only one who lost someone in the last battle."

She smiled at him, her expression understanding. "It's okay."

"Still ... I should have checked in with you. We're both handlers, after all. We need to look out for each other."

Anna let out a watery laugh and wiped her eyes a little. He wasn't sure if she was crying or rubbing the sleep out of her eyes. She laid her head on his shoulder for a second. "It's all right," she said again. "I know what it's like to lose yourself to grief."

He closed his eyes. That's exactly what had happened. He'd been lost, wandering around in a crushing sadness until Sunny had come crashing into his world and forced him to live his life again. "Thanks for putting up with my crabby ass for the last twenty-five years," he said to the air handler.

This time, Anna's laugh was more genuine. "That's

what family is for," she said.

They stared at the horizon for a few minutes, comfortable with each other and the silence. Anna reached out and touched the vase he still cradled. "Are you finally ready to let Dara go?"

Feeling lighter than he had in years, Sloan nodded. "It's not fair to Sunny for me to keep clinging to Dara's memory."

A gentle breeze stirred around them and Sloan recognized the taste of Anna's magic on his tongue. He uncapped the vase and released Dara's ashes. "Goodbye," he whispered as the ashes disappeared into the air, floating toward the forest Dara had always loved. "You'll always have a place in my heart."

Anna's hand crept into his and he held it tightly for a few seconds. "Sunny will be a great partner," she said softly.

He squeezed her hand. "Thanks. And thanks for staying with me while I did this."

Sloan breathed in and felt like he was ready to conquer the world. He wished he could erase some of the pain Anna must still be feeling. "Have you let go of Addison?" he asked quietly.

Her smile was sad when she shook her head. "I'm not quite ready. I think I'm afraid to let him go."

"Why?" he asked.

She shrugged again. "I think I'm afraid if I let him go completely, I'll be lonely. His memory keeps me company, you know?"

He did know. He sent a few silent prayers heavenward. One was a prayer of thanks for allowing him to find his new love, Sunny. He would always be thankful she came into his life. Another was a prayer for Dara's eternal happiness. And the last prayer was one for Anna. He didn't know exactly what he should pray for on her behalf. Should he ask for her to find someone to love? In the end, he just prayed for her to be at peace.

He tugged on her arm until she was pressed against his side and turned so he could rest his chin on the top of her head.

The sun came up slowly, turning the sky a fiery orange. It reminded him of Sunny's flames. In that second, his heart stopped beating to keep him alive and began beating for his Sunny.

* * * *

It was the absence of something warm next to her that woke Sunny up. Even before she opened her eyes she knew the pillow Sloan normally used would be cold. Sure enough, the sheets next to her were cool; although, they still carried Sloan's scent.

Her stomach growled and reminded her it had been twelve hours since she'd eaten. It was imperative she get breakfast and coffee if she didn't want her stomach to digest itself. The kitchen staff wouldn't be around yet but she could always grab a bowl of cereal and some fruit. She wasn't into all the heavy breakfasts Raven and Leith usually insisted anyway.

She was determined to work the whole day on summoning her flame and manipulating it into a deadly weapon. She hadn't forgotten the hunter that had invaded her hotel room back in Canada. If Leith hadn't been there, she wouldn't have survived. Sunny never wanted to be put back in a situation where she couldn't defend herself, and now she had the means to make sure it never happened. She just had to learn how to wield it.

She took a quick second to throw on some clothes before striding into the hall. Of course, she skidded to a halt in front of Sloan's door when she realized it was wide open. "Sloan?" she called. "Do you want to get some breakfast before we practice?"

She studied her fingernails while she waited for Sloan to answer. When she didn't hear anything, she poked her head in the room. "Sloan?"

He never left his door open. She'd always been curious about his room but he'd never invited her in. It was decorated in cool blues and deep, rich greens. A massive bed took up most of the room. The heavy wood of the headboard and dresser dated the room though. And the art deco mirror was at least a good twenty years old. The wallpaper pasted to the wall behind the armoire sported a faded chevron pattern. The turquoise ceramic vase, sculpted to resemble waves, was something she'd seen in one of the foster houses when she was about ten. It was almost like it had been tastefully decorated back in the late eighties, but hadn't been updated since.

Her curiosity got the better of her and she stepped all the way in. "Sloan?" she called again. She didn't think he was actually in the suite. She couldn't hear any sounds from the shower and his walk-in closet door stood wide open. It made her feel better to call out though. At least that way, she could tell herself she tried her hardest to locate him before snooping.

The carpet was thick and squishy under her feet. Yeah, the decorations in the room had to be at least a couple of decades old if the shag carpet was any indication. And, holy moly, how big was his bed? She would probably need a step stool to get in the thing. The bed probably came up to her hips at least.

She approached the bed, determined to find out how huge it really was, when something lying near the edge of the mattress caught her attention. It was a framed photo. Picking it up, she glanced down at it and nearly gasped. The woman was positively stunning. Gorgeous, even. She must have been Sloan's wife.

Sunny felt positively drab next to the woman in the photo.

Carefully, she placed the photo back on the bed and crept out of the room.

She trod heavily down the stairs and into the kitchen, hoping to find the room empty. Her hope was dashed when she spied Matthew sitting at the scrubbed table. He drank from a coffee mug and looked about as down as she felt. "Hey," she mumbled as she trudged into the kitchen and helped herself to a cup of coffee.

She could feel Matthew's gaze on her as she moved around the room and waited for him to admonish her for drinking caffeine. When he didn't say anything, she looked at him with a raised brow.

Shrugging, Matthew took another sip from his cup. "You look like you could really use a pick-me-up," he said, apparently understanding her silent question.

She grabbed a box of sugary cereal Raven had started stocking just for her, and poured a generous helping into a large bowl. She carried it with her to the table and grabbed the milk, adding it to her morning sugarfest. At least it had calcium. Besides, it wasn't like Matthew was going to judge her. "You okay?" she asked Matthew.

"Yeah. I've got a lot going on at work and it's starting to catch up with me, that's all."

The tone of Matthew's voice was off and his answer didn't sound very convincing at all, but she let it go. She'd get it out of him later. Plus, he didn't look like he wanted to talk about what bugged him anyway.

She crunched into her cereal, grateful they were in the kitchen and not the dining room like they normally were for meals. If was far less formal here and she didn't feel the need to be polite. At least she managed to chew with her mouth closed. "Can I ask you something?" she said after swallowing.

"Sure." Matthew sounded a little relieved to be talking about something else.

"Will you tell me about Sloan's wife?"

Why was she doing this to herself? She must be a glutton for punishment.

Matthew looked at her with a sympathetic expression but started talking. "Well, I was only two years old during the last battle. And actually, my family wasn't even at the battle. But from what I've heard, Dara was quite an extraordinary witch. She had remarkable control over her magic and could do as much with her power as Sloan, even though it wasn't nearly as strong as a handler's magic."

The milk on her cereal suddenly tasted curdled and she put down her spoon. Here she was, struggling to manipulate a single flame to her will while this dead woman had had it all. She didn't have it in her to hate the woman though. Sloan had loved her, which said something about her. He wouldn't love someone so deeply if she was a bad person. He certainly wouldn't still be grieving for her after twenty-five years if she was horrible.

Wow. Dara had been beautiful and talented. Everything she wasn't. There was no way she could compete with Sloan's memory of his dead wife.

Matthew squeezed her hand a little and she glanced over at him, unable to hide the tears threatening to spill. "I'm right there with you. Leith..."

He trailed off, looking helpless, and she understood he really did know what she was going through. "God, we're quite the pair, aren't we?" she said through a couple of sniffles. "We should do an ice cream night."

He chuckled. "I have a better idea. Let's meet one night this week and drown our sorrows in booze. There's a pub in town that serves the best cocktails."

She tried to imagine Matthew nursing a brightly colored drink from a margarita glass and failed miserably. "You drink girlie things?"

"No. I'm more of a scotch on the rocks man. But I thought you might enjoy a good tequila sunrise."

Her heart loosened a little. It was good to have a friend. "It's a date. When do you want to go?"

Matthew pulled out a small black day planner and flipped it open. "Well, I'm going with Raven and Leith—" the blond man's name left Matthew's mouth with a small whimper, but he kept talking like nothing happened—"to meet the dragons tomorrow night. How about the day after?"

"Sure," she said immediately. It wasn't like she had anything pressing on her schedule. She was only trying to learn to control her magic so that when the next battle happened, she didn't end up dead. It wasn't anything that couldn't wait.

Matthew smiled and penciled the date into his book. "Seven o'clock okay?"

Before she could respond, Leith stumbled into the kitchen, looking distinctly rumpled, as if he'd just rolled out of bed. He headed straight for the coffee without saying a word and poured himself a large cup.

Matthew made a show of checking his watch. "Look, I really have to get to the office. I'll see you at the pub if I don't run into you before."

He rushed out of the room, leaving a very bemused Sunny. She glanced at the clock on the wall. It was only seven in the morning, way too early for any sane person to be dashing off to the office.

Then again, she could completely understand his desire to avoid Leith. The last thing she wanted to do was face Sloan right then. Not that she had much of a choice.

He was her trainer and she couldn't really hide from him.

Sighing, she got up and dumped her now mushy breakfast down the drain and left, mentally preparing herself for a day spent with her one-sided love interest.

Chapter Sixteen

Holy crap. This place was huge. Sunny clambered out of the limo, thanked the woman who'd driven them, and then stared at the massive rock face that housed the dragon prince's lair. She spun around and grabbed Raven's hand, making his arm jerk as she nearly jumped around in her excitement. "Thank you so much for letting me come," she gushed.

A warm arm wrapped around her middle and gently pulled her away from Raven. "Don't break the man's arm off," Sloan commented, his irritated tone completely at odds with the tender way he held her.

Matthew joined them, looking up at the dragon's lair with an expression of awe. "I know these are part of the same cliffs I suggested searching, but it seems totally different up close than they were in the aerial photos."

Sunny nodded, aware her mouth hung slightly open at the amazing sight. How the dragons had kept humans from finding their lair, she'd never know. The entire face of the cliff was carved like a giant palace. The ocean crashed feet from the entrance and at high tide, it would lap right up against it.

Leith started muttering about pompous ass dragons as he climbed out of the car and Sunny goggled at him. Didn't he realize the woman who'd driven them here was probably a dragon? She could have Leith barbecue if she wanted?

Luckily, the driver smiled slightly, as if she was used to hearing such words.

Soon, the little group of MacAlister witches were gathered a short distance from the cave's opening. Sunny took stock of what was going on, trying to control her excited reaction a bit. She, Raven, Leith, Sloan and Matthew had all come to meet the dragons. Out of all of them, she and Matthew seemed the most excited, but there was something sort of peculiar with Raven.

Before she could question him on why he looked almost giddy, a huge shadow fell across them and she swung her head upward, gasping at the sight that met her eyes. A giant green dragon flew overhead, circling a few times before plunging headfirst into the ocean.

"Dragons swim?" Matthew blurted, looking as astonished as Sunny felt.

Their driver smiled again and shook her head. "Not really. But we do like to fish."

As if the dragon had been waiting for a cue, it exploded from the water with a massive fish clamped in its jaws.

"Show off," Sloan said loathingly.

Sunny poked him in the side without taking her eyes of the magnificent beast as it disappeared among the cliffs. "Be nice."

"Yes," Raven agreed, slinging an arm around Matthew's shoulders even as he gave Sloan a quelling look. "You didn't have to come."

"Yeah," Matthew said, shrugging out from under Raven's arm. "If you were just going to be miserable the whole time, why did you even come?"

Sunny had to hand it to the lawyer. He knew exactly what to say to Sloan to get him to stop muttering. Sloan had never expressly said anything about why he insisted on coming with them when he so clearly wanted to be somewhere else, but she had a feeling it had something to do with her reaction to finding out about the handsome dragon prince.

She should have been a little insulted by his obvious jealousy with regards to the lizard prince, as Sloan had taken to referring to him as, but she actually found it a little endearing. At least she knew he wanted to be with her.

"We should go in," the woman said. "Prince Gareth will be impatient to meet with you."

"An impatient dragon is never a good thing," Raven muttered under his breath.

Sunny looked at Raven quizzically. It sounded like Raven knew about impatient dragons from personal experience. Of course, Raven had dealt with the dragons before, but his words hinted at a much more intimate connection with them.

She couldn't help but wonder if Raven had a relationship with one particular dragon. She couldn't help but notice the unfocused, slightly misty look Raven got in his eyes whenever someone mentioned the dragon queen. Could there be something more between them than just a working association?

Then again, if Raven had a romantic relationship with the queen, he and Leith wouldn't have been looking so hard for the dragons. And the steady stream of women Raven seemed to entertain on an almost daily basis was hardly indicative of a man in love.

Sunny glanced around at the men as they followed the woman into the palace. Matthew looked at Raven consideringly, as if trying to puzzle out the hidden meaning behind the man's words.

Leith's expression didn't give anything away. Of course, it was highly possible that Leith really questioned Raven's dating habits. Sunny doubted very many people looked past the constant stream of women Raven brought home to see the man was actually miserable.

She looked up at Sloan to see if she could decipher

what he was thinking, but instead of looking at Raven, Sloan's eyes had widened and his mouth hung open slightly.

Swiveling her gaze from Sloan's face to the cave they were entering, Sunny felt her own jaw drop. If she'd thought the outside of the cliff had been impressive, she was floored by the interior.

Instead of plain gray stone, the walls were covered with brightly covered tapestries. There were beautiful carpets on the ground and gigantic fireplaces with roaring fires. She wandered over to the hearth, trying to figure out where it vented, since it wasn't spewing smoke into the room.

There were electric lights in the ceiling, computers scattered around the room and a television in one corner. Clearly, there was a generator somewhere because there was no way they were on the grid.

"Do you have any questions? I've lived here all my life and I can probably answer anything you ask."

An absolutely gorgeous man stood in front of them. He smiled at them, an amused expression on his face. Good lord, the man was like a Greek god come to life. He was tall and muscular without being too bulky, and had cheekbones that could cut diamonds. His damp hair was cut short and fell in thick waves just above one of his eyes. And speaking of his eyes ... God, his eyes. They were such a bright green, it almost hurt to look at them.

As attractive as the guy was, Sunny's magic still tugged toward Sloan and she stepped a little closer to him, even if it was only to reassure the already tense man she was only interested in him.

It turned out she didn't need to show Sloan that her interest lay solely in him because Mr. Greek god seemed to only have eyes for Matthew. The man's smile, while it encompassed all of them, seemed to be directed at the lawyer, and she repressed a little squeal of girlish excitement.

Of course, Matthew, as fair as his complexion was, had turned a dusky shade of pink and seemed to have lost control of his mouth, because it kept opening and closing without actually forming any words.

Leith brushed against Sunny's side as he stepped forward, but she didn't think he even realized. He made a beeline for Matthew and placed a hand on his shoulder. "Please excuse our Matthew. He still has the curiosity of youth."

If Leith had said that about Sunny, she would have had some very choice words for him. Matthew certainly handled it better than she would have. "What is your hang up about my age?" he shot back lightly. "I get that I'm not five hundred years old, but I'm not a child."

Sunny nodded once in agreement and towed Sloan over so they stood next to Matthew. Leith rolled his eyes but didn't say anything more. Instead, he jerked his head at Raven as Mr. Gorgeous left the entrance with a wink. "Keep an eye on Matthew before he offends someone," Leith hissed at Raven.

Raven's eyebrows shot up but he stepped closer. "He's fine," Raven commented.

Leith let out a clearly irritated breath and stalked farther into the cave. Sunny chewed on her bottom lip, trying to figure out what was going on with him. She looked at Matthew, who stared at Leith's back with a confused expression.

Despite his reassurance that Matthew's attitude was fine, Raven did turn to them with a serious look. "I want you two to be careful," he said, pointing to both Matthew and Sunny. "Dragons might parade around in human form, but remember, they are most definitely not human.

They think differently than we do. Sloan has dealt with dragons before, so he already knows this, so I'm confident he'll be on his best behavior."

Sunny nodded, but the image of the great beast plunging into the ocean wasn't one she'd soon forget.

The young woman who'd picked them up smiled again. "Please, follow me."

They followed her down a hall and into another huge room, where a long table was set up. Twelve people were already seated around the table, including Mr. Gorgeous, who sat at the head of the table.

Their escort stepped forward and addressed the room. "Your Highness, my lords. May I present Raven and Leith MacAlister, Matthew Samuels, Sloan Shirer and Sunny Kerrigan of the MacAlister witch clan."

Mr. Gorgeous rose from his seat and nodded. "Thank you, Leandra. You make take your seat."

The woman bowed low, her long hair nearly brushing the floor. "Thank you, Your Highness."

Sunny's gaze jumped to the man at the head of the table. Of course, the prince would be seated at the head of the table. He was gazing in her direction with a knowing expression on his face, but he didn't seem to be looking at her. His eyes were fastened on Matthew, who stood beside her. She glanced around the table as discreetly as she could, searching for any sign of who might be the queen. Nobody stood out to her. Then again, it wasn't like she had a whole lot of experience in identifying dragon royalty.

Suddenly, Matthew bowed low, in the same manner as Leandra. Sunny fidgeted a little, unsure of what to do. Bowing certainly seemed appropriate enough, seeing as she was in the presence of royalty. But no one else in their group bowed, so she bent down in a stiff half bow.

Leith's tutting caught her attention and she straightened to see him giving her and Matthew an exasperated look. "You doona need te bow," he said in his suddenly thick brogue. "He is no' yer prince. He is an ally, nothin' more."

She smirked a little even as she allowed Sloan to steer her toward the table. Apparently, Leith's brogue and proper English became extremely pronounced when it came to Matthew. Could the man be hiding feelings for the young man?

The lawyer, on the other hand, seemed extremely irritated. "It doesn't hurt to be respectful," he shot back. He was quiet enough that only he, Sunny and Leith would be able to hear what he said. "We *do* want them to support us in the war, after all."

Leith didn't answer. Instead, he took Matthew's elbow and guided him to an empty chair about halfway down the table, right next to the one Sloan nudged her toward.

Matthew never made it to the chair, though. "I would like Matthew to sit next to me," the prince said with authority.

Sunny poked Matthew in the side when he didn't move. "Matthew," she whispered, feeling wicked. "Go up and sit with the sexy man." She waggled her eyebrows at him suggestively.

"Shut up," Matthew whispered back as he blushed again. But he did make his way to the head of the table and sat down in the chair to the right of the prince.

The table was promptly set with a beautiful meal. There were roast chickens, steamed fish, colorful vegetables and tureens of thick, rich gravy. It smelled divine but Sunny was far more interested in watching the interaction between Matthew and Prince Gareth.

She tapped Sloan's knee excitedly under the table when the prince placed a slice of cake on Matthew's plate.

"Try this, sweet one."

Sloan slipped his hand over hers and forced her to stop shaking his leg. "Sunny, you're going to dislocate my hip. Why are you so excited, anyway?" he whispered.

"Matthew seems so lonely and sad. I'm happy someone is giving him the attention he deserves."

Sloan linked his fingers through hers and squeezed her hand lightly. "I expect being in love with Leith is no easy thing. And I agree, the prince does seem to be rather taken with our Matthew. I guess that's a good thing. As long as Prince Gareth doesn't eat him, that is."

She giggled, happy that Sloan seemed to have relaxed a little now that he knew the prince had his sights set on someone else. He even seemed to be enjoying himself.

Her good mood wilted somewhat when Leith started talking. "I would hardly call Matthew sweet. He's a legal shark, a master computer hacker and is highly accomplished in several forms of martial arts."

Sunny cocked her head and frowned. While Leith's words were all compliments, they came off kind of condescending and she got the idea he was rigidly controlling his accent. "What's his problem?" she whispered to Sloan.

Sloan shrugged and forked another bite of chicken into his mouth.

However, far from being put off, the prince looked intrigued. "Perhaps fierce one suits you better. Going back to our conversation from before, do you have any questions?"

This time, the prince glanced around the table, his eyes settling on Sunny as his mouth quirked up in a tiny grin.

"How do you leave the palace at high tide?" Sunny

blurted immediately. "I assume the cars are stored some-where above the water line?"

The prince nodded and placed his dessert fork on the edge of his plate. "Yes. There is a cavern we store the cars in which is above the tide line. And if we need to leave before the tide goes back out, we fly."

"I saw," Sunny replied, remembering the green dragon plunging into the sea.

"There's a cave we take off from. Would you like to see it?" Prince Gareth asked, smiling indulgently at her.

How many times would she ever have this chance again? "Yes, please."

The prince rose to his feet, gesturing for Sunny to fol-low him. "Would anyone else like to join us?"

Sloan's big body brushed against hers as he stood as well. "Actually, I would love to see a little more of the palace."

Sunny was pleased to hear that Sloan sounded genu-inely interested in seeing the palace instead of just accompanying her to make sure she didn't stray.

The prince nodded. "Very well. And I would love to show Matthew, as well."

Sunny suppressed another giggle as Matthew blushed, again, and rose to his feet. "I'd be happy to tag along."

Across the table, Leith made to stand, but Raven stopped him with a hand on the forearm. "We're fine. We'll stay here and help set up for the meeting."

Sunny grinned at Raven, who winked at her. Appar-ently, she wasn't the only one who thought Matthew and Prince Gareth should get to know each other.

"As you wish," the prince said. "If you will all follow me." He reached out and gently tugged on Matthew's el-bow when the man remained frozen to the spot.

Sunny linked arms with Sloan and followed the prince and Matthew down the corridor. They ambled through several winding halls, up at least four flights of stairs and down some more corridors. She hardly paid any attention to where they were going, though. She was far too busy looking around. When she wasn't admiring the portraits on the carved stone walls, she was trying to figure out if the prince was naturally touchy-feely or if he was flirting with Matthew. She was leaning toward flirting. Nobody accidently brushed against someone else that much by accident.

Finally, the prince led them to a gigantic cavern carved out of the side of the cliff. The scent of the sea floated in the room and the bright moon was clearly visible from the entrance. "This is where we take off from."

Sunny walked right up to the edge of the ledge and looked down. They were at least fifty feet above the ocean. The view made her dizzy and she stepped back, colliding with Sloan's warm body. He anchored an arm around her waist and pulled her against him tightly. "Don't want you to fall," he whispered into her hair.

She leaned back against him and sighed, staring out into the night. The bright stars and the sound of the crashing waves combined to make a romantic atmosphere. Sloan rested his chin on the top of her head and she slid her hand over his.

Behind them, she could hear Matthew and Prince Gareth talking quietly. "It must be amazing to fly," Matthew said.

The two men joined them at the exit, standing so close together, their shoulders were touching. "It is. Don't most witches have the ability to fly?"

Matthew shook his head. It was Sloan who answered. "No. Most witches can dissipate through doors and such by using a spell. They can use the same spell to travel long distances in short periods of time, so it's often mistaken for flying. It's a common misconception among other paranormals. Handlers don't have that ability though. Except for the most basic of spells, we're pretty much limited to what we can do with our specific element."

Gareth nodded and looked over at Matthew. "You, though, are not a handler, correct?"

Matthew stared out at the night and nodded. "Right."

"So," Prince Gareth continued. "You've used spells to travel. I imagine the sensations is much like flying."

Sunny's throat tightened and she gazed at Matthew with concern. He'd never said anything about how not having magic made him feel, but when he'd told her on the plane, he'd sounded almost ashamed.

Matthew stared straight ahead. "I was born without magic."

Sunny prepared herself to jump to Matthew's defense. Even Sloan tensed behind her. She was sure Matthew had experienced his share of pity over the years, having been born into a clan of witches but with no magic.

"Maybe I could take you flying one day," the prince said, immediately gaining her utmost respect for putting her friend at ease.

"How would that work?" Sloan asked.

Prince Gareth answered, but only had eyes for Matthew. "I would shift into my dragon, and you would climb on my back."

"It sounds rather ... intimate," Matthew said, echoing Sunny's exact thoughts.

"It is. Extremely." The prince's voice was low and rumbling, almost like a purr.

If the sexual tension between Matthew and Prince Gareth got any thicker, she and Sloan would have to hack their way out of the room with a machete.

Poor Matthew was nearly the color of a tomato. Sunny had never seen him blush this hard, or this frequently.

And, judging by the amused look on Sloan's face when she craned her neck to look up at him, neither had he.

The lawyer looked like he was trying to figure out something to say. "Were you the dragon who went fishing earlier?" he finally said.

The prince's face broke into a wide grin. "I'm glad you noticed. I saw you get out of the car, and I knew I had to get your attention."

"You were amazing," Matthew said.

The expression on the prince's face softened into something far more sensual. "Thank you. I've been told I'm pretty amazing at other things too."

The prince was definitely flirting with Matthew. Sunny would have taken Sloan and gone back to Raven and Leith, except she was pretty sure she'd get lost along the way, so she settled for keeping her mouth shut.

Matthew seemed to ignore fact she and Sloan were present. Either that or he didn't care. "Are you gay?" he asked bluntly.

The prince, obviously ignoring her and Sloan's presence, stepped closer to Matthew and continued speaking in that low, seductive voice of his. "Dragons don't define sexuality the same way your people do. We do not believe we should be limited to loving only one gender."

"So in other words..." Matthew's voice trailed off with a soft gasp, and Sunny risked a glance over at the two men and had to stuff her fist against her mouth when she saw the prince nibbling a little on Matthew's ear.

"Wow," Sloan breathed in her ear. "Prince Gareth certainly moves fast, doesn't he?"

Sunny nodded and held her breath, trying to be as quiet as possible.

"In other words," the prince said once he pulled back

from Matthew slightly, "dragons find both males and females attractive. Also, you should know ... dragons are very bold. When we see something we want, we rarely take long to claim it."

"Your Highness," Matthew said softly.

"Call me Gareth," the prince replied.

"Gareth," Matthew repeated.

"My name sounds beautiful on your lips," the dragon murmured just loud enough for Sunny to hear.

Sloan started coughing, and Sunny made a show out of patting his back. "We should get back to the meeting," she said loudly.

She felt bad for interrupting. The last thing she wanted to be was a cockblocker, but she was pretty sure Matthew had forgotten she and Sloan were in the room, and she wasn't sure if Gareth really cared they were there.

Matthew was still a bright shade of red, and Sunny wondered if he was ever going to go back to his normal complexion.

Prince Gareth, however, was still looking at Matthew with obvious lust. "I can summon someone to take the two of you back to the main hall, if Matthew wants to see a little more of the palace."

Sunny was about to accept Prince Gareth's offer. She even considered suggesting he take Matthew on a tour of his bedroom, but Matthew was already shaking his head. "We really should get back to Raven and Leith."

The prince smiled charmingly and spoke again. "I do hope you'll consider coming back for a more *thorough* tour another day."

"He will," Sunny said brightly, patting the slightly stunned Matthew on the arm.

The action seemed to snap the lawyer out of his momentary stupor. "Maybe," he said softly.

Sunny could practically see the image of Leith dancing in Matthew's brain, but there wasn't much she could do about it.

Gareth clearly wasn't fazed by Matthew's answer at all. Not when he slung his arm around Matthew's shoulder and grinned. "Playing hard to get? I have a feeling I'll enjoy the chase."

Sloan linked his fingers with Sunny's, and she swung his arm playfully as they followed the two men back to the main hall.

When they arrived, they found the dishes had been cleared and pens, pencils and pads of papers littered the table. The place now looked more like a board room than a dining room. Sunny and Sloan sat back down in their previous seats. Matthew headed for an empty chair between Raven and Leith, but Gareth steered him to a different seat. "I would prefer you to sit here, fierce one," Gareth said, pulling out the chair next to his.

Matthew sat and looked over at his leader, shrugging. Raven smiled and waggled his eyebrows. He was clearly going to grill Matthew on the way home. Leith didn't even glance up. He simply stared down at the table, scowling. Sunny frowned at Leith's attitude. What the hell had crawled into his dinner and died?

Gareth sat down and picked up a pen, tapping it against the table. "Now that the meal is finished, it is time to get down to business. Raven MacAlister, have you recalled your clan as per our agreement?"

Sunny suddenly clued into something that had been right under her nose. Matthew had been making calls to clan members, asking them to come home. He'd just told her that his parents had already put their house up for sale in Australia, and once they had everything in order, they would be moving to clan grounds.

They were building an army. An army composed of MacAlister witches and, hopefully, the dragons.

Now wasn't the time to question Raven, or even Leith, about the upcoming events. Not when Gareth began speaking again. "I'm sure by now, you have all realized that the queen has not joined us."

The room was silent and Gareth tapped his pen again. There was no playfulness in his expression anymore. Now, he looked like the very image of a cold, hard-hearted army general. "She is our second condition."

Sunny didn't miss the way Raven leaned forward and focused all his attention on the prince. "What about Queen Niya?"

Gareth eyed Raven. "She disappeared the day of the last witch battle," he answered. "We believe there are two possibilities. I suspected she had a secret lover for a number of years before the battle. Did she run away with her lover?"

"I knew your mother very well," Raven said, looking offended. "She loved her people. She would not run away with a lover."

Gareth nodded slowly, looking at Raven with a strange expression. "I agree. The more plausible, but far less happy reason my mother would have disappeared would be because she was kidnapped."

This time it was Leith who spoke up. "Who do you suspect?"

"The vampires. They dropped off the face of the earth the same day." Gareth looked troubled. "We've been searching for her since she failed to return, but we can only do so much in our dragon form before we're noticed by humans. In exchange for helping us find our queen, we will join you in battle when the time comes."

"We'll do it," Raven said immediately.

"Huh," Sloan muttered quietly. "That's weird. Raven

doesn't usually make decisions like this without having Matthew do at least a little bit of negotiating."

"Wait a minute," Matthew interrupted.

The prince's cold expression thawed slightly. "Yes, Matthew?"

"What if we haven't found your queen before the battle? Will the dragons still fight by our side?"

"Good man," Gareth said with an approving tone. "Yes. As long as genuine effort is put into the search for my mother, the dragons will battle with you."

Matthew nodded slowly. "I'll put something in writing, and you can have someone look at it and see if you agree."

The prince rested his elbows on the table and steepled his fingers. "I make the legal decisions regarding the dragons," he said. "So I'll meet with you at a later time to discuss your agreement."

Matthew nodded as he jotted in his notebook. "I can have something ready for you in the next few days. Is there some way I can contact you to set up a meeting?"

Prince Gareth pulled out a business card and handed it to him. The card was a heavy stationary with black script writing, spelling Gareth's name and the words "treasure hunter." There were two numbers printed on the card and one number handwritten with blue ink. "Call the third number. It's my personal cell."

Matthew extracted one of his own business cards from his pocket and scrawled something on it. "Here, this is my number."

Sunny was beyond excited. She couldn't wait to tell Anna all about how the prince flirted with Matthew and how flustered Matthew was. She was already planning on asking their driver if they could stop at a bakery on the way home so they could have something sweet to snack on while they chatted. Maybe she could talk Matthew into joining them.

Abruptly, Leith pushed back his chair and stood up. "We need te get goin' before the tide comes in," he announced, his accent full and heavy.

Gareth saw them to the exit, where the same woman was waiting to drive them back home. Leith waited exactly three seconds after they got into the car before starting in on Matthew. "What were ye thinkin', goin' off alone with a dragon? Especially since I've told ye more than once that I've felt an increase in unfamiliar magic nearby."

Matthew glared at Leith. "Geez, Leith. You told me that, with the increase in your magic, it's hard to tell how close the unfamiliar magic actually is. What's with you?"

"Are ye that desperate, Matthew? That filthy dragon was eyeing you like he was a bee and you were the flower. And what were ye doin' with him for so long?"

"Why is it your business?" Matthew shot back. "It's not like you have any claim on me."

Sunny felt like she was watching a tennis match. One would lob a question or an insult, and the other would respond immediately.

But Leith's reaction was a little over the top. He was acting like a jealous lover. Maybe there was more to it than she realized. Leith certainly seemed protective, almost possessive of Matthew at times. She'd witnessed the number of times he'd brushed up against Matthew at meals.

Leith growled and grabbed Matthew's wrist. Matthew didn't pull away and Sunny had to give him credit for standing his ground. "What, Leith? Tell me how you feel right now," Matthew demanded.

Leith leaned forward until his mouth was barely a centimeter from Matthew's.

Sunny held her breath when Matthew raised his free arm and caressed Leith's cheek.

"Say the word," Matthew whispered. "Say the word and I'll tell Gareth we will only be business associates."

Sunny's lungs were beginning to ache from holding her breath for so long, but she didn't want to chance interrupting this very intense moment. She felt like she was eavesdropping, but there wasn't anywhere else for her to go. Especially since the driver had already started the car's engine and eased onto the beach.

"Matthew..." Leith's voice sounded a little desperate, like he needed to say something and just couldn't find the right words.

Heartbreaking for Matthew, Sunny watched as Leith reached up and gently removed Matthew's hand from his face and muttered a spell. Less than a second later, the blond witch had disappeared.

Matthew dropped his hand into his lap. "Well," he whispered. "I guess I got my answer."

Sunny was about to climb over Sloan's legs to give the lawyer a hug, but Sloan beat her to it. He wrapped his arm around Matthew's shoulders and pulled him close. Raven patted Matthew's knee. "It'll be fine," he said softly.

Matthew swallowed and nodded jerkily before leaning his head against Sloan's shoulder for a brief second before sighing and pulling out a business card from his breast pocket. Sunny recognized it as Gareth's card.

"He's a good man," Sloan said, nodding at the card. "And he's clearly interested in you."

Matthew didn't say anything, but he did run his thumb over Gareth's name.

Sunny almost couldn't believe her eyes. She'd never seen Sloan and Matthew really interact with each other.

They'd always acted more like acquaintances than anything else but here Sloan was, comforting another man, a gay man at that, without a second thought. It showed her an entirely new side of Sloan.

Touched, she linked her fingers with Sloan's and squeezed gently. Sloan squeezed back and continued whispering to Matthew.

Chapter Seventeen

Sunny slid on to the bar stool next to Matthew and grinned. "Thanks for inviting me," she said.

Matthew smiled back and signaled for the bartender. "I thought you could use a break from all the training," he answered.

"Oh, you have no idea." She placed her order and munched on a few peanuts. "This is the first time I've been away from the castle at night since I got here."

A brightly colored cocktail was placed in front of her, and Sunny lifted her glass to salute Matthew. "What should we cheers to?"

Matthew picked up his own glass and clinked glasses. "Friends," he said.

"Friends." She almost choked when the strong alcohol trickled down her throat. "Jeez, is this liquid fire or what?"

Snorting, Matthew shook his head. "You should know. Is this really the first time you've been away from the castle for a night out?"

Nodding, Sunny took another sip of her drink, this time prepared for the sensation. It went down easier this time around and made her stomach feel all warm and fuzzy. "Sloan pretty much has me practicing all day long. We did come to town once a couple of weeks ago to stretch our legs, but we didn't stay late."

"If I'd known it was your first night out, I would have taken you somewhere else." A plate of warm bread and something she couldn't identify was delivered to them and Matthew selected a slice of bread. "Want some?"

Sunny eyed the plate suspiciously. Matthew had recently taken great delight in trying to trick her into eating gross things. He was quickly turning into the older brother she'd never had, and she'd learned to ask for clarification on what was being served before she took a bite. "If that's haggis, I'm outta here," she warned.

A quick burst of laughter escaped Matthew. "Ah, I have you paranoid, do I? No, it's just brie and mushrooms baked inside some pastry."

"Oh. Then yes, I'll try it."

They ate in companionable silence for a few seconds and Sunny relished the change from the heavy meals the men at the castle seemed to insist on. "I haven't seen you around lately," she said after she'd swallowed a bite of the velvety cheese.

Matthew shrugged. "I've been spending most of my days in my office here in town. These days, I pretty much use my room at the castle to sleep and nothing else."

Sunny couldn't help but wonder if the young man was trying his best to avoid a certain blond giant but didn't say anything. "What kind of law do you practice" she asked instead.

"Business mostly," he replied, wiping his mouth on a napkin before taking another swallow of his drink. "Most of my days are spent negotiating Raven's business deals."

Business deals? The leader of the clan actually worked? Oh, the man was busy enough. He was constantly dealing with clan stuff but she'd never actually seen him work outside the castle.

Matthew laughed again and tapped her nose with a single finger. "You should see your face. Yes, Raven works. Who do you think pays to run the castle and the clan?"

She hadn't really thought about it before. Now that she actually did think about it, she felt a little guilty. She hadn't offered to get a job to pay for her room or board or anything. She'd taken it for granted they would take care of her while she trained.

"Hey," Matthew said softly. "I know what you're thinking. Raven is a financial genius, okay? He has more than enough to support all of us in style for the next five hundred years, and that's if he stopped investing right this second. He'd rather you train your magic than worry about contributing financially when he doesn't need you to."

"Are you sure you can't read minds?" she asked. He'd certainly seemed to be able to pick up on what she'd been thinking about for the last half an hour.

Matthew popped another bite of cheese into her open mouth and grinned. "Nope. Not a drop of magic running in these veins, I promise. You're just easy to read."

"Really?" She'd never had anyone say that to her. Usually they said they couldn't figure out what she was thinking, let alone how she felt.

"You're an open book, my dear."

Snorting, Sunny threw a peanut at Matthew and laughed as it bounced off his impressive chest. "You sound as old as Leith when you talk like that."

Matthew's face fell for a second and Sunny groaned inwardly. Shit, she wasn't usually so insensitive. "Sorry," she said softly.

The young man was quiet for a few seconds before clearing his throat. "Don't worry about it. It's true. And I have to get over him."

Sunny brightened. "Yeah. Let's get you a date," she exclaimed as she scanned the pub.

"I appreciate the sentiment, but I doubt you'll find many gay men here. I've been thinking about asking Prince Gareth out for dinner." He lowered his voice and leaned close. "I have it on good authority that dragons tend to swing both ways."

She giggled. It was nice having someone her age to hang out with. Even Anna, who was the youngest handler next to her, had been raised in another generation. "Maybe I could convince Raven to let me go too."

"Yeah right," Matthew said with a smirk. "Like Sloan would let you come."

"Hey," Sunny said, trying her best to sound affronted. "Sloan is my trainer, not my boss. And besides, we argue all the time. It would be nice to have a conversation with an attractive man without worrying about how moody he might get."

"Are you saying I'm not attractive?" Matthew shot back. "Stop trying to horn in on my fun. Besides, I know exactly how you and Sloan like to resolve your arguments."

"I have no idea what you're talking about," she huffed, trying to hide behind her glass.

"Uh huh," Matthew said with another smirk. "I heard your argument in the hall the other day. I don't think that particular bathroom has ever been used for make-up sex before."

Sunny giggled even as a blush worked its way up her neck and across her cheeks. Two days ago, they hadn't been able to wait until they got back to one of their rooms and Sloan had fucked her on a random bathroom counter. It had been really late and neither of them had really considered the fact that they might be disturbing someone else. "Sorry," she muttered once her laughing fit had stopped.

"Don't be. It was the most action I've had in months," Matthew teased. "And apparently, Sloan is really, *really* good in the sack."

"Oh, God," she groaned and buried her face in her

hands. "This is so embarrassing."

Matthew laughed long and loud, and she only looked up when it trailed off. The expression on his face wasn't a good one. "What?" she said.

"Oh, holy fuck," he whispered. "We are in so much shit."

Spooked by Matthew's scared expression, Sunny looked around the pub. She didn't see anything out of place. In fact, except for a few new patrons, there was absolute nothing different. "What's the matter?"

"Leith told me a couple of days ago he'd felt an increase of unfamiliar magic, but with his power growing, he had trouble determining how close the strange witch was. Well, I think one of the guys who just walked in is from the Takahashi clan. We need to get out of here."

Her heart instantly started racing. Trying to look as casual as possible, she accepted Matthew's help off the stool and stuck close to him as they moved for the door. "I borrowed one of Raven's cars. It's down the street a little," she said.

The tall Asian man by the door shifted a little and Sunny tensed, but he turned away from them instead. Matthew tugged her through the door and held on tight to her hand, digging in his pocket with his free hand for his cell phone. "My car's right here. We'll take mine, and Raven and I will come for the other car tomorrow."

Sunny watched as he hit the number one on the phone's keypad and raised it to his ear. "Who are you calling?" she asked as they hurried to Matthew's car.

"Raven," he said as he cradled the phone between his ear and shoulder and unlocked the car, shoving her inside.

Apparently, Raven picked up right away because Matthew started talking almost immediately. "Rave, I'm pretty sure Sunny and I ran into a Takahashi witch at the pub. We're coming home right now."

He tossed the phone to Sunny. "Here, keep Raven on the line until we get to the castle," he ordered as he stuck the key in the ignition.

Sunny raised the phone to her ear. "Raven?" she asked. She wasn't really sure what else to say. She was nervous but then again, maybe Matthew had made a mistake.

"Don't worry, sweetheart," Raven crooned, clearly trying to keep her calm. "Matthew will get you here fast and we'll get everything sorted out."

Of course, the car would have to start in order for them to get anywhere. "Shit," Matthew muttered.

Sunny glanced over and saw his hands shaking so badly, he could barely grip the key, let alone turn it in the ignition. "Maybe I should drive," she said, already halfway over the seat.

Matthew ignored her and finally succeeded in starting the car. "Raven," he called out, even though Sunny was still holding the phone against her ear. "I remembered where I saw the Takahashi before. He was in the picture you showed me from thirty years ago. The one you said was probably a Takahashi handler."

"Fuck," Raven breathed. "Get out of there now."

Before Sunny could relay the message, there was a deafening thump from behind and the car lurched.

Sunny dropped the phone on the seat and looked over her shoulder. The Asian from the pub crouched on the trunk, staring in with a wicked smile.

"Fuck," Matthew shouted. "Raven, get people here now. We're about to become involved in a confrontation."

Sunny reached over and locked the car doors automatically, not that it really mattered. If the guy wanted to get in, he would break the window. "Drive," she screamed at Matthew.

The car shot forward, but a loud screeching sound caused Matthew to jam on the brakes, nearly throwing her through the windshield. Sunny hit the window head first but luckily, she stayed inside the car. She shook her head, trying desperately to stop it from spinning. "Fucking hell," Matthew shouted. "It's definitely a Takahashi handler."

Still dizzy, she fought to understand what was going on. Raven's voice was screaming from the phone, which was on the floor. He hollered about how he, Anna, Sloan and Leith were on their way.

The loud screeching started again and Sunny clutched her head as the sound drove into her brain like a knife. Matthew's put his face in front of her. "We have to get out of the car," he screamed.

She scrambled after him, ignoring the nausea the sudden movement caused, and slid through the opening where the door used to be.

Wait. The entire side of the car was missing, peeled off like the rind of an orange. And if she wasn't mistaken, it took her feet a few seconds longer to meet solid ground than she had expected.

She blinked hard, trying to focus on what was going on but her brain refused to accept the fact that the car was hovering nearly a foot in the air. A chunk of metal flew past her, narrowly missing her head. She heard Matthew's pained cry behind her and spun around to see the twisted piece of metal pin his leg to the ground.

It suddenly hit her that Matthew had no magic and it was completely up to her to protect them.

A protectiveness like she'd never known before welled through her. Matthew was her friend, a real friend. She was sure he wouldn't abandon her, unlike all her other so-called friends in her life. She would protect this man to her very last breath, if it came down to it.

Her mind cleared, all pain forgotten. Moving so Matthew was directly behind her, Sunny eyed the other handler. He'd stopped throwing things at them and eyed her suspiciously. "You look a little small to be the new handler," he called.

She would show him. The ball of fire she summoned was hotter and bigger than anything she'd ever summoned before. She threw it toward the other handler and it collided with a metal shield, presumably the side of Matthew's car.

The feedback from her magic colliding with the other handler's sent vibrations up her arms and the pain in her head, which she'd managed to forget, came back with a vengeance. Still, she held the magic, forcing the flames higher and hotter until the makeshift shield melted.

The magic flowed through her, unchecked, and started to flare out of control. She could hear Sloan's voice behind her, screaming at her to pull the magic back but it was too late. The other handler's eyes widened and he ceased his magic, disappearing from view.

"I have to hold the illusion," Raven shouted.

Sunny was confused. What illusion?

Sloan was suddenly at her side. "Sunny," he said urgently. "Concentrate. Pull back on the flames a little. Raven can only hold the illusion the other handler set up for so long."

She had no idea what everyone was talking about but she did what they'd trained her to do. She emptied her mind of everything but the flames and calmly called it back.

The fire seemed to laugh in her face and instead of extinguishing, it flared even higher. Several cars that lined the streets were completely engulfed and some of the buildings were starting to burn. No matter how much she calmed herself and tried to call the magic back into her being, it ignored her.

"Sloan," Raven croaked. "I can't hold it much longer."

"Anna," Sloan shouted. "We need to call up a rainstorm."

It took a few seconds but Sunny felt the first drops of rain sizzle off her skin. Soon, it was pouring and the flames were slowly diminishing.

With the fire dying out, Sunny was able to take control of her magic again and pulled back on some of the flames. She was sweating and ready to vomit within thirty seconds. Her head felt like it was going to explode and the pressure, which she'd come to associate with a buildup of magic, was staggering.

Next to her, Raven finally collapsed. "Sunny, relax and sit down," he ordered weakly. "Let Sloan and Anna hold the rainstorm until the firefighters get here."

She did as he directed, collapsing next to him and laying her aching head in his lap. People started streaming out of buildings, screaming and calling for the fire department. She finally realized Raven had been holding some sort of magical illusion in order to keep the ruckus under wraps. "You have some explaining to do," she said. "Like why the fuck was that handler able to make things fly around."

Raven looked contrite. "We may have forgotten to mention ... different clans have control of different things. The Takahashi has control of things like telekinesis and mind reading."

Sunny sighed but didn't say anything. Her head hurt too much to process that information right then. She'd figure it out and give the appropriate person hell for not telling her later.

Sirens wailed in the distance, and Sunny managed to push up enough to look for Matthew. Leith was behind him, supporting him even as the younger man clutched his leg. She tried to drag herself over to them, but Raven grabbed her wrist and forced her back to his lap. "Leith will take care of him. You need to stay still and wait for the paramedics yourself."

"Paramedics?" she asked.

"You're bleeding," Raven said, wiping some moisture off her face she'd thought was sweat and rain, and showing her the red liquid on his fingers.

Tears filled her eyes. Now that the initial adrenaline rush was wearing off, Sunny was feeling the effects of the battle. Every part of her body hurt. She didn't want to go to the hospital. All she wanted to do was find a bed, snuggle up with Sloan and sleep for the next two days.

The noise around her increased and two strangers bent over her. "Let's see what we have here," one said.

Sunny tensed but Raven stroked her hair. "It's just the paramedics. Relax."

She knew Raven wouldn't let anyone hurt her. She really did. But everything in her called out for Sloan.

A bright light was flashed in her eyes and she groaned when a shaft of pain streaked through her brain. She could hear the paramedic saying something about a concussion and for her to hold tight while they checked on the other victim.

Finally, Sloan dropped down next to her. He was covered in soot, soaking wet and mad as hell. He was the most beautiful thing she'd ever seen. Her heart skipped a beat as she reached for him. He would shelter her. He would support her. He would take her home and sleep beside her until she felt better.

"What the hell was that?" Sloan whispered furiously.

Sunny blinked. It was not exactly the response she'd been expecting.

"Sloan," Raven said softly.

Sloan's brown eyes snapped with anger. "Your little display of magic nearly killed all of us. Stop playing and grow up, little girl."

"Sloan," Raven said again and this time, it was a clear warning.

She pulled herself up so she sat back against Raven.

"No. Listen up, Sunny. You are a handler. You hold an immense amount of power you clearly aren't ready for. I don't know what to do about you anymore. You need to try harder before you kill yourself. God, I can't even be around you right now."

The water handler stormed off, leaving her reeling in Raven's arms. Sunny turned her face into his chest and started to sob.

Funny how she hadn't realized she'd fallen in love with Sloan until the man had broken her heart.

Chapter Eighteen

Sloan paced the waiting room, trying desperately to stop his hands from shaking. He hated hospitals with a passion. The only thing worse than the white walls of the room were the pale green, lumpy couches. How was one supposed to sit comfortably while waiting for news of their loved one? Maybe that was the point. He wasn't supposed to be comfortable while Sunny and Matthew were suffering.

Anna was curled up in a corner of one of those couches, picking at a string sticking out of the hem of her T-shirt. "They'll be okay," she said quietly, not meeting his eyes.

Sloan nodded but didn't stop his pacing. He needed to move if he was going to have to be confined in this room. He still hadn't gotten over the sight of Sunny, pale and bleeding, fending off the Takahashi handler all by herself. She'd been surrounded by flames and for one second, it had been magnificent.

When the Takahashi handler had taken off into the night, he had been torn between chasing the man and going to Sunny.

Then the fire had roared out of control and not even the fire handler could survive being engulfed in flames. He'd called down the rain so fast, it had made him dizzy and still, it hadn't been enough. Anna had had to stir the currents, creating a massive storm, in order to even control half of the flames.

Sunny had eventually gotten a hold of the fire and called it back into her, a process he knew could be painful if the magic had gotten too big. He'd just about lost it when she'd collapsed but had enough presence of mind to make sure any fire near his loved ones was extinguished before he'd rushed over to her.

She'd been so still for a moment, he thought she'd passed away and his heart had died right there with her. The pain was immeasurable, more acute than anything he'd ever experienced. His capability to function had been stripped from him, and he knew Raven or Leith would have to take him down, to kill him, because without Sunny, Sloan would go rogue in a matter of days. The destruction he would have caused on his rampage would have been catastrophic.

Then she'd moved, trying to pull herself up. And he'd made the biggest mistake of his life. Instead of confessing his love for her like he should have, he'd let his rage at himself, at his inability to protect her when she'd needed it most, come leeching out, and the words had been out of his mouth before he could stop them.

The look on her face had confirmed it wasn't his brightest move ever, but he hadn't known how to fix it. Before he could even attempt to apologize, the paramedics had come back and loaded her into the back of an ambulance. Raven had shot him a deadly look and climbed in the back with her, leaving him to follow with Anna.

Raven had met them in the waiting room, and other than confirming he hadn't been hurt, hadn't spoken a word to Sloan since.

The door swung open, and all three of them looked up hopefully. Leith staggered in, looking like he'd been through a war. His long hair was loose around his shoulders and there were lines of stress around his eyes that hadn't been there a few hours ago. No one had been able to pry him from Matthew's side.

Raven shot to his feet and rushed to Leith. "Matthew?"

Leith covered his face with his hands for a few seconds. "His leg is broken badly," he answered with a thick brogue. "He's goin' into surgery now. But the doctors assure me he'll be fine."

Raven slumped suddenly and Leith caught him. "Raven," Leith gasped as he bore Raven's weight.

Sloan rushed over and supported his leader from behind. "Rave, are you hurt?"

The leader slowly straightened. "Sorry, I'm just relieved. Matthew means a lot to me."

A low growl ripped through the room, but everyone ignored it. Leith bowed slightly. "I'm sorry for the outburst, Raven. I know ye'r quite fond of Matthew."

Leith strode away to the window and stared outside. Raven sat back down, and Anna moved closer, patting his hand. Sloan resumed his pacing.

Another half an hour passed and there was still no news about Sunny. Sloan was starting to think he was going to go mad. No one had said a word since Leith had come in and the silence was starting to get to him. "Raven, we need to put a push on Sunny's training," he said to break the silence.

Leith didn't say a word, not that Sloan had expected him too. Anna nodded and started pulling on her shirt's loose string. It was Raven's silence that surprised him. "Raven?"

The leader didn't even look at him. "Now's not the time," he answered.

Sloan stopped his pacing and stared at Raven. "I thought we might want to make use of our time."

Again, Raven didn't answer.

"What, are you not talking to me or something?" he spat, trying desperately to figure out what his leader was thinking.

Raven finally looked up at him and there was murder in his eyes. "I'm too angry with you to say anything right now."

Apparently, Raven had been paying attention when Sloan had gone off on Sunny.

The awkward silence settled over the room again and this time, it was Raven who started pacing.

Finally, a nurse entered the room. "Are you all here for Sunny Kerrigan and Matthew Samuels?"

"Yes," Raven said, coming to a stop in front of her.

Sloan's mouth dried and his heart attempted to beat its way out of his chest. He stood up and hurried to stand next to Raven. Even Leith joined them, his mouth drawn in a tight line.

The nurse flipped through her notes. "Right. Mr. Samuels is leaving the recovery room now. He came through the surgery just fine. You'll have to wait until he's sufficiently awake, and then the doctor can give you more details on exactly what was done."

Leith's quick exhale was audible through the entire room, and Sloan glanced at the man he'd known all his life. It was clear the man was relieved, and he couldn't help but wonder if Leith didn't return Matthew's feelings, even a little.

His attention was dragged back to the nurse when she started talking about Sunny. "Ms. Kerrigan is just finishing up with her MRI."

Eventually, they were allowed to go to the rooms. Leith and Anna went to Matthew's room while Sloan went with Raven to Sunny's.

Sunny looked so small and fragile lying in the hospital bed, and all Sloan wanted to do was carry her home, drape her in bubble wrap so she couldn't get hurt again, and never let her out of his sight.

Raven approached the bed. "Sunny? Love? How are you feeling?"

A small, pale hand reached for Raven's and Sloan was struck by how tiny she actually was. Her personality and strength always made her seem so much bigger. He edged a little closer to hear her answer. "My head really hurts and I'm pretty nauseous, but I'm alive, so that's all that matters, right?"

Raven leaned over her and stroked her hair. "I'm so glad you're okay. You've gotten under my skin, love, and I would be sad if something happened to you."

For a moment, Sloan wondered if it was possible to actually turn green from envy, because jealousy buffeted him so hard, he wanted to smack the other man around.

And then, his heart broke with her next words. "Can someone else train me?"

For the first time since his wife's death, Sloan wanted to cry, but he understood her request.

Sighing, Raven stroked her hair again. "Sorry, Sunny, but Sloan is still the best person to help you train." Raven's silent "even if he's a prick" rang in the quite room.

"Okay," she said softly. "How's Matthew?"

If Raven was surprised by her easy agreement, he didn't show it. "He's got a broken leg, but he'll be fine."

She nodded and then winced, grabbing her head as if it was about to roll off her shoulders. Sloan flinched himself. He wished he could take the pain for her, but that was impossible. So was crawling into bed with her, if the looks Raven was shooting him were to be trusted.

"I'm glad," she whispered. "Tell him I'm sorry about his car. It was a really nice one."

Raven's laugh was a little watery. "I'll buy him a new one, don't worry. Just get better. I'm going to check in on Matthew now. Will you be okay by yourself?"

What the hell was Raven talking about? She wouldn't

be by herself. Sloan was going to stick to her like glue from now on. "I'll stay," he clarified.

Of course, both of them ignored his statement. "I'll be fine," she said. "I'm going to sleep."

"Okay, love," Raven said. He stroked her hair one last time before turning away and glaring at Sloan. Raven pointed at Sloan's chest and growled. "Don't do anything stupid."

Sloan simply hung his head. Nobody liked to treated like a child, but he deserved it.

Raven bumped into him hard on his way out and Sloan did his best not to react. Instead, he crept over to Sunny's bed and pulled a chair closer. "I'm sorry, Sunny," he said, the words tumbling out of his mouth surprisingly easy considering he didn't make a habit of apologizing very often. "What I said was uncalled for, and I didn't mean it."

She blinked up at him and a single tear eased from her eye and down her temple. "It's fine," she said.

He could tell from her voice that it was anything but fine, but there was nothing else he could do. Not right now, at least.

He watched over her as she fell asleep, and collapsed into the chair next to the bed. He felt utterly hopeless and worse, he had no idea how to fix what he'd so callously broken.

The door eased open and Anna slipped in, closing the door behind her with a soft click. She threw Sloan a look full of disgust as she settled on the side of Sunny's bed. Anna reached out and tucked a strand of Sunny's hair behind her ear in a motherly fashion.

She didn't say a word to Sloan, but she didn't have to. Sloan could feel her disdain from across the room.

Finally, he couldn't take the silence anymore. "I know," he whispered. "I know I screwed up. I was so scared, I didn't know what to do."

The sweet, agreeable Anna he'd always known seemed to have disappeared. "So you decided to take it out on her, when she was hurt and vulnerable?" she asked, scorn positively dripping from her voice.

Sloan couldn't help the flinch. "I really don't know what came over me." Except he did know. He knew exactly why he'd reacted the way he had. When he'd seen Sunny trying, and almost failing, to hold off a Takahashi handler on her own, he felt a deep sense of urgency. He'd known at that moment he was utterly in love with her. And he was about to lose her.

A darkness had nearly overwhelmed him, and it had been all he could do to make sure he didn't harm any of his clan mates while he controlled his magic, forcing it to rain instead of flood the whole damn street.

When it was over, he looked over at Sunny, only to find her sprawled on the ground with her head in Raven's lap, as still as death itself.

His sanity completely shattered and for a brief second, he'd been about to drown the whole lot of them, including himself. Then he'd seen her chest moving, seen her mouth move as she spoke to Raven, and he'd lost it.

Anna shook her head and went back to petting Sunny's hair softly, exactly like a mother would. He supposed she was almost old enough to be Sunny's mother and he knew Anna had certainly developed some fond feelings for the fire handler. "You need to get a hold of yourself," she advised, but her voice wasn't as harsh as it had been a few minutes ago. "Look. Why don't you go and visit with Matthew? I know he'd like to see you and, somehow, I don't think Sunny will be very happy if you are still here when she wakes up."

That probably wasn't a bad idea. "You'll stay with Sunny?" he asked.

"Of course," she replied, not even sparing him a glance.

He sighed. He supposed he deserved the slightly cold shoulder she was giving him. "What room is he in?"

Anna gave him directions on how to get to Matthew's room and he left with one last reluctant glance at Sunny's sleeping form.

Matthew's room was fairly quiet when he finally found it. He could hear Raven and Leith talking softly, not loud enough for him to hear the actual words, but by the serious tone, he guessed they were probably talking about increasing the speed with which they recalled the clan. He stepped inside as Matthew was blinking up at them all, looking adorably confused. Sloan doubted the man would appreciate being called adorable though, even in this state, so he decided to keep the thought to himself.

"Wha..." Matthew mumbled.

Before either Raven or Sloan could do anything, Leith was at Matthew's side. Sloan watched as Leith bent over Matthew. "Are ye finally awake, lad?"

Matthew nodded and tried to say something, but his voice only came out as a croak.

Leith shook his head and pressed his finger to Matthew's lips. "Hush, lad. Let's get ye some water."

Sloan glanced around the room and found a plastic pitcher perched on a small table. A quick look told him it was, indeed, filled with water. Grabbing a paper cup from the dispenser on the wall, he poured the water, added a bendy straw that lay next to the pitcher and handed it to Leith.

Leith held the cup for Matthew and directed the straw into the man's mouth. He waited patiently for Matthew to drink his fill, murmuring occasionally about how he should slow down so he didn't choke.

Finally, Matthew cleared his throat and rested his head against the pillow again. "Is Sunny okay?"

"She has a concussion, but she'll be okay," Sloan answered.

Matthew fixed him with a misty stare. "Why aren't you with her?"

"Anna's with her, don't worry," he answered, not wanting to admit he'd messed up so badly.

Matthew nodded but stopped quickly. "What's the matter?" Leith asked. "Where does it hurt? Lad? Should I get a nurse? Sloan, make yerself useful and get the doctor." Leith's tone bordered on panic.

"I'm just dizzy," Matthew said softly. "So, apparently that guy was a Takahashi handler after all."

"He was," Raven answered. "Something was off though. I know him from before. He was always the most reasonable Takahashi. I don't know why he would have launched an all-out attack. I'm not sure what happened."

"He did seem a little crazy," Matthew said. "Can someone raise the bed for me so I can talk to you properly?"

Leith obliged him and Matthew groaned as the back of the bed was raised. "Why am I so dizzy? I didn't hit my head, did I?"

"That would be the anesthesia still working its way out of your system," a nurse said from the doorway. She smiled at them all as she hustled over to the bed and stuck a thermometer in Matthew's mouth. He held it obligingly under his tongue and straightened his arm as the nurse took his blood pressure. She removed the thermometer and stuck it back in the machine.

Leith closed in on the bed again, looking slightly panicked. "Why are ye takin' his blood pressure and his temperature? Is there something else wrong with him?"

The nurse shook her head. "No. It's just procedure."

"Is it all right if I come in?"

The voice was familiar, and Sloan spun around to see Prince Gareth standing in the doorway.

"Oh, Your Highness. Of course you can come in. If the patient says it's okay, that is," the nurse said with a smile.

"Come on in," Matthew invited.

There was something so regal about Gareth, Sloan couldn't help but give a little half bow.

The prince spared him a smile, but only had eyes for the man on the bed. "Your nurse is one of my dragons. She called me as soon as she figured out who you were," Gareth said.

Sloan swiveled his head so he could watch Matthew. The young man blushed and looked as if he didn't quite know what to say or do. Leith, meanwhile, had risen from his place by Matthew's bed and stalked across the room, like he was about to kill something. Sloan had the nasty idea that Leith was currently plotting how to murder a certain dragon.

Matthew started speaking again. "Unfortunately, Your Highness, I'll need a few more days than I originally thought to get our agreement written down."

The prince strode across the room and sat down on the edge of Matthew's bed. "I'm not here because of our alliance. I'm here to make sure you're all right."

"He's fine," Leith said.

"No offence, Leith MacAlister, but I would rather hear that from Matthew," Prince Gareth said, not even bothering to look in Leith's direction. In fact, he never removed his gaze from Matthew's face.

Sloan wondered briefly if anyone in the world had ever blushed as hard as Matthew was blushing right then. He was about to make the joke, to try and lighten the atmosphere a little, when Matthew groaned. "Shit, my leg hurts."

The nurse, who had been scribbling on her clipboard in the corner, hurried over and handed Matthew something. "This is so you can self-administer your pain medication," she explained. "Just press the button and it will release a dose of morphine into your I.V."

Raven approached and gently removed the wand from Matthew's hand, pressing the button for him. "It will work soon, right?" the leader asked.

The nurse nodded. "Yes. There are no limits on it right now. Use it. When you're discharged, it will be back to over-the-counter stuff for you."

"Don't worry," Raven said. "I'll make sure he uses it."

Matthew nodded. "Don't worry. I'm not a masochist. I'll take the pain meds while I can get them."

"Good," Prince Gareth said. "I don't like to see you in pain, Matthew."

Matthew cocked his head a little. "Can I ask you something?"

The prince nodded and shuffled around until he sat next to Matthew, leaning back against the mattress with him, their shoulders brushing.

"Why do you call me Matthew but you call everyone else by their full names?"

Sloan exchanged a panicked look with Raven. One did not question a dragon about their traditions, especially not one of the royal family. If anything happened to Matthew because of the breach of protocol, it would be on their heads, because not one of them had thought to instruct the young man in dragon etiquette. Raven rushed forward and tried to capture the prince's attention. "You Highness," he said, "please forgive him. He didn't mean any offense."

"He's fine," the prince said dismissively. "Matthew, dragon protocol dictates that we are very formal with people we respect."

Sloan could see Matthew trying to work through what Gareth's words meant. "Does that mean you don't respect me?"

The young man's words were slightly slurred, indicating that the painkillers were finally starting to set in.

"On the contrary," the prince answered. "I respect you very much. I'm only using your first name as a sign I want to get to know you better. Hopefully, a lot better."

A low growl ripped through the room moments before Leith slammed his fist into the wall. He followed up the action by striding out of the room, muttering about Lothario dragons under his breath.

Sloan looked back at Matthew, who blinked around at the room. "What happened?" he asked thickly.

Gareth sighed and patted Matthew's arm. "Sleep now."

"'Kay," Matthew agreed as his eyes fluttered shut. "But someone needs to check on Leith. Something's off with him."

Sloan stepped forward and bent down a little so Matthew could see him clearly. "I'll go check on him now. Feel better, champ."

"M'not fifteen," Matthew muttered as he fell asleep against Gareth's shoulder.

Sloan left the room and wandered the hall, looking for Leith. He found the man in the waiting room, facing the windows.

Sloan sighed. He and Leith were both idiots. Leith was deeply affected by Matthew; he had been from the first day Matthew had stepped into the castle when he was seventeen. Before the incident, Sloan had always thought Leith only viewed Matthew as a younger brother. Now, everyone in the room could see he was in love with the young man. Anyone except Leith, himself, apparently. Or maybe, the man simply couldn't admit he was in love with Matthew.

Sloan was another story. He was ready and willing to admit to both himself and everyone else, that he was in love with Sunny. He just didn't know how.

Yep. Both of them were complete idiots.

Chapter Nineteen

Sloan sighed when he saw the bouquet of flowers he'd sent to Sunny sitting on the dining room table. This was the third one she'd refused to put in her room.

He was at a complete loss as to what to do next. Obviously, flowers were not the answer. And chocolates weren't the answer either, since he'd found the box he'd sent to Sunny sitting on Raven's desk yesterday.

Sunny had been nothing but polite to him since she'd been released from the hospital. She said all the right words and even smiled at him from time to time, but it wasn't the same. Her smile never reached her eyes anymore and she avoided his touch. Hell, she avoided being in the same room alone with him let alone sitting next to him at meals.

Matthew hobbled into the room and eased himself down into his seat, propping his crutches against the arm of the chair. "Hey, Sloan," he greeted.

Maybe the answer was staring him right in the face. Sunny and Matthew had gotten quite close since she'd come to the castle. He probably knew what he could do to make her forgive him. "Matthew, can I ask you something?"

The young man looked up at him with surprise, and Sloan immediately felt guilty. Matthew had been living here for six years, and he really didn't know the kid at all. In fact, he couldn't remember ever having a conversation with Matthew. They really didn't speak unless they had to.

It served to highlight how far into his depression he

had been before Sunny came into his life. Still, it hadn't been an excuse to totally ignore everything and everyone around him.

He was ashamed of himself. Hell, Dara would have lectured him about his behavior until she turned blue.

"Sloan?"

He blinked at Matthew's voice and forced himself back to the situation at hand. "Sorry. I zoned out for a second."

Matthew smiled kindly. "I've been known to zone out myself every once in a while. What can I do for you?"

He couldn't believe he was about to ask someone more than forty years younger than him for advice on his love life, but it wasn't like he was doing so hot on his own. "I kind of made an ass of myself where Sunny is concerned."

Matthew nodded. "I heard."

Sloan waited for the dressing down Matthew was probably itching to give him. Everyone else in the castle certainly had already torn him a new one.

When Matthew simply waited for him to speak, Sloan was taken aback. "Don't you want to shout at me?" he blurted.

Laughing, Matthew shook his head. "You've probably already had the lecture from at least three people. You don't need to hear it from me."

Sloan relaxed. Matthew didn't look particularly upset, just curious. "Thanks. I appreciate it."

"No problem. Now, about Sunny?"

Trust a lawyer to cut right to the issue. "Well, I've been trying to get her to forgive me, but I can't seem to get it right."

Matthew frowned. "Forgive you? She told me she forgave you before she was discharged."

"I know. But it's just not the same between us. I know

I shouldn't expect it to be the same," he rushed to say before Matthew could point it out, "but I wish she would at least give me a chance to apologize properly."

"No offense, but I don't think the way to her heart is through flowers and chocolate. The candy was pretty tasty, by the way," Matthew said with a smirk.

Sloan couldn't help but laugh. "Glad you approved. So, do you have any advice?"

"Yep. Get those peanut butter cups from North America next time. They're freaking delicious."

Despite his serious question, Sloan was delighted with Matthew's come back. The kid was smart, witty and had a great sense of humor. He'd have to make an effort to spend more time with Matthew in the near future. He had a feeling Matthew would be a hoot to party with and also be able to hold his own in a debate.

"Funny. I'll keep that in mind. But about Sunny?"

Matthew flashed him a grin before getting serious. "The thing is, she knows you didn't mean what you said. But it wasn't what she needed to hear right then. She probably felt like you'd abandoned her, especially when you threw Dara in her face."

The whole idea that Sunny might have felt abandoned was an eye-opener. She had talked with him briefly about her past and how she'd been raised in a series of foster homes. It wasn't inconceivable that she would feel deserted when he'd lost his temper, when what she'd needed him to be was supportive. "Man, I really messed up."

Matthew struggled to his feet, or rather his foot, and grabbed his crutches. "Look. Just spend some time with her. Watch movies, talk to her ... hell, why not try reading the same book so you have something to discuss."

He pursed his lips and thought about it. They hadn't

really done much but sleep together since they met. Watching a movie with her could be fun. And reading a book wouldn't kill him. And maybe showing her he cared by spending time with her would be more effective than telling her with flowers and candy. "Thanks, Matthew. I'll do that."

Matthew propped the crutches under his arms and winked at him as he straightened. "No problem. I have a vested interest in you and Sunny getting back together."

"Yeah? What's that? Do you and Raven have a bet on if Sunny and I get back together or something?"

"No. You're much more pleasant to be around now that Sunny's here. You're not all doom and gloom anymore. But a bet is a good idea. I'm going to find Raven and talk him into making one." Matthew limped in the direction of Raven's office. "I'm betting on you, by the way."

Sloan watched Matthew leave the room, feeling much happier than he had when he'd first woken up to see the flowers he'd sent Sunny sitting on the table. He strode over to his laptop and fired up a search engine to look for recent movie releases.

Opening a new tab, Sloan pulled up an American candy store. Matthew was going to get his peanut butter cups as often as he wanted for the rest of his life.

*

Sunny watched from the library window as Sloan left the castle. She wished he'd quit sending her flowers. They were beautiful and thoughtful, but they made her feel guilty because she couldn't seem to get past his words.

"What's vexing you, lass?" Leith said from behind her.

She spun around, clapping her hand to her pounding heart. "You scared the shit out of me," she said. "Don't sneak up on me like that."

Leith raised an eyebrow and wandered over to the cappuccino machine in the corner. He made his selection and pressed the brew button. "I made plenty of noise. You weren't paying attention."

The machine beeped, signaling that the coffee was ready. Leith took a sip and sighed. "As much as I detest technology sometimes, I have to say, this coffee is so much better than it was when I was young."

Sunny grinned and plopped into a seat next to Leith. "What did you do all those years ago? Grind your coffee beans between a couple of stones?"

"You know, anyone else would treat me with respect," he commented lightly.

She giggled and patted his hand. "I've figured you out."

Leith rolled his eyes but didn't refute her comment. Instead, he went back to his original question. "What's bothering you?"

Sunny felt her smile fade and she fidgeted a little in her seat. She really didn't know how to explain what she was feeling so she didn't say anything at all.

Leith didn't seem to need her to speak. "You're still punishing Sloan."

"No," she denied with a gasp. "I forgave him as soon as he apologized."

"But you've been going out of your way to avoid him since you came home, and he's been bending over backward to try and make you happy again."

Leave it to Leith to bluntly tell it like it is. "I know." And she did. She just didn't know what to do about it.

Leaning forward, Leith pressed a soft, paternal kiss to the top of her head. "Do you really forgive him for his words?"

She nodded before letting her forehead rest against his collar bone for a minute. If Raven was becoming like an older brother, Leith was definitely becoming a father figure. She wrapped her arms around his shoulders and hugged him, despite their awkward position.

Leith squeezed her in return before pulled back. He tilted her head back with his fingers under her chin and looked her straight in the eyes. "Then do you think perhaps something else is going on?"

Sighing, Sunny nodded again. "How do you know me so well?"

Leith smiled softly and ruffled her hair. "I told you before. You remind me so much of my Elizabeth. I'll leave you to your thoughts. But I want you to think about Sloan and why you're so reluctant to let him get close again."

He stood up and strode to the door, pausing to look at her over his shoulder. "I'm not saying you have to forgive him. I am saying you should understand if you're pushing him away because of what he said or if you're pushing him away because you're afraid of something."

She closed her eyes and leaned her head against the back of her chair. Leith was right, of course. She wasn't upset about his words. She'd gotten over those long ago, recognizing he'd said them in the heat of the moment.

It was the fear of being abandoned stopping her from moving forward.

She'd always thought she was a strong, independent woman. But it turned out that when she was confronted with the possibility of happiness, she was a wimp who ran away from the fear of being hurt instead of fighting for her happiness.

It wasn't fair to her and it certainly wasn't fair to Sloan.

The man in question shuffled back into the castle and stopped hesitantly in the library doorway. "Sunny. Hi."

It was now or never. Ignoring the sudden flight or fight instinct that churned in her gut, urging her to run, she smiled. "Hi, Sloan."

The hopeful smile that bloomed on his face proved she'd made the right decision. "I got a couple of movies. What do you think about taking a break from training to-day and having a movie marathon? We can grab Anna, and Raven could probably be talked into watching at least one of them."

Crossing the floor, Sunny took the bag from Sloan and peeked inside. It was full of romantic comedies. They weren't something she could picture Sloan picking out on his own, so he'd probably had her in mind when he chose them.

Touched, and a little amused since she would have been thrilled with a horror movie marathon, she reached for Sloan's hand and laced her fingers with his. "Let's watch them alone."

She walked with Sloan to the media room, never letting go of his hand. She couldn't guarantee she would be able to move past her fear, but, damn it, she would try

.

Chapter Twenty

"Crap."

Sloan's voice drifted from the kitchen, startling Sunny. Curious, she wandered in the direction of the man's frustrated voice and poked her head in the room.

She didn't know whether she should laugh or not. Thick, black smoke rose from a frying pan as he used his magic to pour water on its contents. He muttered under his breath, something about never cooking again.

Finally, she couldn't hold her curiosity in anymore. "Um, Sloan?"

The man in question spun around, spatula in hand, and stared at her with wide eyes. "Hi, Sunny," he answered.

"What are you doing?" She tried to peek around his body at the stove, which still issued copious amounts of smoke, but he blocked her.

"Making dinner."

Sunny raised her eyebrows and took another step forward. She deked left and scooted around his right side to gaze down in the pan. An unidentifiable piece of ... something ... sat in the middle of the metal surface. Whatever it used to be, she was pretty sure it wasn't supposed to look the way it currently did.

Sloan joined her and poked at the burnt mass with a fork. "It's chicken."

Sunny had to clear her throat a couple of times to prevent herself from laughing. He looked so forlorn. "Why are you making dinner?" she asked when she finally got a hold of herself. "I heard Raven mention something about pizza."

He smiled at her a little sheepishly. "I kind of talked him into ordering out so I could make dinner for you. But, as you can see, I can't really cook."

Her heart gave a little flutter. None of the men she'd dated in the past had ever cooked for her. Touched, she made a resolution that she would choke down every single bite.

Luckily, Sloan poked at the meat and sighed. "This isn't fit for beast, nor man. I guess we'll have to join the others for a slice of pepperoni."

"I think Raven ordered a couple of supreme pizzas. And, if you really want to eat pizza with them, that's fine, but you have to eat the mushrooms. I don't like them."

"Deal," Sloan agreed. "I wish we could have had a quiet dinner. I even bought wine." He gestured toward the small room off the kitchen, where Anna sometimes attempted to sew.

Curious, she wandered over and looked inside. Her fluttering heart melted. The small table was covered by a pristine white table cloth. A bottle of white wine sat chilling in a silver ice bucket and two tall candles were standing in matching silver sticks.

By the time she'd gotten a hold of herself and returned to Sloan's side, he was scraping the pan clean. "The pizza should be here by now," he commented.

"You know what?" she said, putting her hand on Sloan's wrist. "I don't feel like pizza. How about pasta? I could really go for some fettuccini alfredo."

Sloan placed the pan in the sink with a clatter and grimaced. "I don't know if we have the ingredients."

Sunny reached into a cupboard and extracted a jar of sauce and a bag of macaroni from the depths, setting them down on the counter. "It's not exactly gourmet, but it will taste good."

He looked at her skeptically but bent down to retrieve a pot from under the oven. His pants stretched tight across his ass and she took the opportunity to ogle it without having to hide her interest.

"Are you sure you want macaroni with jarred alfredo sauce?" he asked as he straightened.

"It's perfect."

They worked together and were sitting at the table, candles lit and wine poured, after half an hour. The pasta was overcooked and the sauce tasted like the jar instead of parmesan cheese, but she didn't care.

"Would you like to go back into town?" Sloan asked after a sip of wine.

"Now?"

"Sure, why not? We could get some ice cream for dessert. I have very fond memories of that ice cream stand."

She took a sip of wine to cover her smile. The image of him with the little girl tugged at her soul. "Do you ever want kids?" she asked.

Sloan smiled and his gaze focused somewhere over her shoulder, as if he was looking into the future. "Yeah. I do. How about you?"

She was only twenty-five years old. She had lots of time to have a family so there was no rush. But she already knew the answer. "Yes. How many do you want?"

"I'd love as many as you want," he said without missing a beat. It might have sounded like a line coming from someone else, but she could tell from his expression he meant every word. If she wanted to stop at one, he'd be fine but if she wanted five or six, he'd be okay with that too.

Let's not get ahead of ourselves. She wasn't ready to set herself up for possible heartbreak from the man, let alone have his kids. And yet, the picture of him cradling a small baby close to his wide chest did funny things to her.

"So, what do you think? Do you want to go into town?"

Sunny looked down at her plate of soggy macaroni swimming in white sauce and her half full glass of wine. "No. Actually, I was thinking we could spend the evening in."

"Really?" Sloan's voice clearly reflected his surprise. "It's been a while since we've gotten away from everyone."

Obviously, Sloan had not caught on to her meaning. "I didn't mean we have to spend the evening with everyone."

Understanding slowly dawned on Sloan's face. "Want dessert upstairs?" he asked, grabbing a plate with a slice of chocolate cake and waggling his eyebrows suggestively.

She smiled and pushed away from the table. "As long as you let me have the last bite of cake."

Sloan surged to his feet and blew out the candles. He linked their fingers together and started leading her toward the back staircase once meant for servants. "Of course. As long as you eat it off me."

* * * *

Sunny spit out a strand of hair and stretched. The beam of sun shining through the small crack in the curtains told her the sun was high in the sky. Her stomach growled, not content with last night's meal, and she turned her head, searching for her lover. The bed next to her was cold, and she couldn't hear anything from the bathroom.

Last night had been amazing. The effort he'd put into the dinner, the conversation about children, and the fact that he'd spent all night long making sure she was satisfied had brought her to the very edge of love. All it would take was one little nudge and she would be unequivocally in love with him.

She sat up and stretched her arms over her head. Looking around, she found a folded piece of paper on the pillow Sloan had been using.

Curious and more than a little anxious, she picked it up. Didn't people write notes when they wanted to break up?

Taking a deep breath, Sunny opened the paper and nearly cried when she read the words.

My beloved Sunny,

As I sit here, watching you sleep, I know I need to drive home just how much I love you. So these are my promises to you.

I will kill all the bugs, even the centipedes that creep me out.

I will always let you have the last bite of dessert, even if it's my favorite crème brulee.

I will let you choose the radio station in the car, even if it's country music.

I promise to kiss every burn, every slammed finger, and all the table-bumped hips.

I will always let you sleep on my chest, even when you drool.

I will thrust harder and faster. I will be rough when you want and tease you when you don't.

I'll leave you random gifts.

I'll make the bed every morning.

I will always need you.

I will love you.

I will love you.

I will love you.

You own my body, my heart and my soul.

Yours,

Sloan

Sunny blinked the moisture out of her eyes, scared

she would splotch the paper if she wasn't careful.

The bedroom door eased open and Sloan stepped inside, bearing a huge tray. "Good morning," he said, setting the tray down on one of the dressers. "How are you?"

"Fine, thanks," she answered, her voice slightly husky from the unshed tears. She cleared her throat and glanced up at him.

His eyes flicked toward the paper in her hands and he seemed to understand the cause of her distress. "Um, I brought breakfast."

She cleared her throat again and slid his note under her pillow. "Did you make it?" she asked.

Sloan chuckled and shook his head. "No. I got everything from the dining room this morning. I brought you some bacon, eggs and a slice of toast. I thought about bringing up some yogurt, but there was only pineapple."

She was surprised he knew she didn't like pineapple, but didn't say anything.

He set up a tray across her lap and placed a plate in front of her, chatting brightly while he settled next to her with his own breakfast.

Gazing at Sloan, she opened her mouth when he offered her a strawberry.

She glanced down at her meal and felt her eyes misting up again. Forget being on the edge of love. He'd just provided the nudge she needed to tumble head first into love.

Chapter Twenty-one

A thick cloud of black smoke clogged Sunny's throat, and she waved her hand in front of her face, coughing to clear her lungs. "Crap," she choked.

"Sunny," Sloan groaned. "You have to at least try to control your magic."

Crossing her arms over her chest, she stomped her foot in frustration. "I *am* trying, damn it."

"Okay. Let's try again," Sloan said slowly.

Sunny shook out her hands and stared down at the charred grass. Her magic had massively increased in power since her confrontation with the Takahashi handler. She could barely manage a small ball of fire anymore, let alone raging flames. It was the reason why they had to move their training to the pasture half an hour away instead of the small field near the castle. She'd taken to setting the woods on fire and she was pretty sure a forest fire would attract some unwanted visitors.

"Sunny," Sloan called again. "I know you're trying to release some of the energy before you summon your fire, but you won't have time to shake out your hands in a real battle."

She rolled her eyes. Like she hadn't figured that out when the Takahashi dude was hurling chunks of metal at her with his mind. "Okay. We're trying to create steam."

"Right," Sloan said with a nod. "So you need to control the temperature of your fire so my rain evaporates mid-air. Try not to let things get too hot, or we'll end up setting the field on fire. Again."

Sunny appreciated Sloan's use of the word *we*, she really did. She knew it was her fault the field kept going up in flames. She also knew Sloan was trying his best to make up for what he'd said immediately after her confrontation with the Takahashi handler. He'd been attentive and sweet ever since she'd come back from the hospital.

"Okay," she said again, and re-focused her attention on the situation at hand. "Let's do this."

She waited until he'd called down the rain before summoning her fire. She let it dance in her palm until she felt she had some kind of hold on it and then concentrated on heating it until the rain hitting the ball of flames sizzled. The drops of water started to explode into steam. "It's working," she said, excited.

"It is," Sloan responded. "Let's increase the amount of rain."

"Do it," she said, emptying her mind and concentrating on her fire.

It promptly started to pour. Water streamed down her face, plastering her hair to her face. Calmly, she manipulated the fire in her hands, slowly increasing the heat until they were completely engulfed in a cloud of steam. "We're doing it," she squealed. She felt like jumping up and down.

"Okay," Sloan said, moving closer. "Now, I'm going to focus the water into one large stream. Because this is a much stronger manipulation of our magics, you're going to have to let me help focus your fire. Kind of like how I let Anna move my water when we're creating a storm."

She nodded and tried to calm her racing heart. She relaxed as much as she could as Sloan narrowed the diameter of the stream of water until it fell in a single, colossal column. Directing the ball of fire under the water was the easy part.

Once the two magics merged, however, things got a little out of hand.

Something seemed to move in the back of her mind, as if there was another presence in her head. Instinctively, Sunny knew that presence was Sloan, and he would have complete access to everything in her. Her memories, emotions, fears and desires were no longer private. There was no way to hide those parts of her core and, far from being comforting, it terrified her. It made her vulnerable, defenseless, something she swore she'd never be after the last foster home and she panicked.

Her magic responded to her distress and roared to life. It felt like a living thing, like it was trying to protect her, and immediately surrounded her in a wall of flames. The grass around her began burning immediately and instead of creating steam, Sloan's water merely extinguished the fire, resulting in another belch of black smoke.

She yanked back on her magic as hard as she could and managed to draw most of the flames back into her. Her body hummed with power and she jumped around for a few seconds, trying to re-absorb the magic.

Sloan stood next to her, breathing heavily. She could tell he was trying desperately not to blow up. "You have to stop fighting me," he said lowly. "Something is blocking you from letting us move forward."

"I know," she cried in frustration. "But I have a hard time letting people in."

Sloan let out a breath and clenched his fists. "Why? Why can't you let me in?"

The truth came tumbling out before she could stop it. "After my parents died, I grew up in a series of foster homes. But the foster families always decided I was too much work, and I always got transferred to another home. Or locked in the psych ward because they were convinced there was something behind my behavior."

She took a breath as the feelings came flooding back.

"Do you know what it's like to have your stuff piled in garbage bags, like you're trash, and dropped off at another strange place?"

She hadn't even been aware of the tears rolling down her cheeks until one dripped on her hand. She wiped them away angrily, irritated because she'd let herself get this worked up over something from the past. And the soft look on Sloan's face didn't help. She didn't want to be pitied, damn it. Sunny turned away and scrubbed at her face.

Sloan didn't take the hint. He turned her around again and pulled her into his arms so her head rested on his chest. She tried to hold herself stiff, to not give in to the comfort he offered, but the warmth of his hug chipped away at her resolve and she found herself reluctantly relaxing.

"Every time you got used to something, started caring for someone, it got taken away from you. Am I right?" he said, summing up her entire childhood with one simple sentence.

How could something that felt so complicated be put so simply into words? "No," she said stubbornly.

Sloan pulled away slightly and bent down a little until she was forced to look him in the face. She didn't look him in the eye though, instead staring at his chin. "Sunny, sweetie, you know we'll never abandon you, right? You belong with us. You belong with me."

She blinked and fought back another wave of useless tears. She knew Sloan really believed his words. She just couldn't get over her fear of having someone she loved taken away from her again.

She didn't want to think about it anymore. Sloan had gone out of his way to show her he loved her. If he left her, it wouldn't be his choice.

And the thought of losing Sloan made her tremble.

She linked her arms around Sloan's neck and pulled him close, needing to be close to him. She needed to feel his skin, needed to have him deep inside her. She *needed* to feel like she was one with him. "Let's take a break," she murmured.

Sloan's eyes showed his hesitancy, his desire to keep prodding at her issues until they were resolved, but she caught his lower lip between her teeth and tugged gently.

Groaning, Sloan picked her up and carried her to a soft, unblemished patch of grass. The ground was spongy at her back, comfortable. Perfect for what they were about to do.

She reached for him, needing him close. He kissed her, slow and sweet, like he had all the time in the world. Maybe they did have all the time in the world. His mouth coaxed hers gently as she gave in to his unspoken request without hesitation. She loosened her arms from around his neck and skimmed her hands down his back. His skin was hot, the heat radiating from under the thin cotton of his T-shirt. His muscles rippled under her touch, a shiver working its way through his body. "Sunny," he said with a sigh.

Their clothes seemed to disappear like magic. She looked up at Sloan, about to comment, when she noticed the little smirk playing at his lips. "Neat trick," she said. "You'll have to teach me some time."

"I just didn't want to stop kissing you."

Sunny shuddered when Sloan began planting warm, wet kisses down the side of her neck. "Please tell me you didn't magic away the condom."

Sloan raised his head slightly. "I'll never be caught without a condom again." He reached over her head and fumbled in the grass for a moment before pulling his arm back and waving a shiny foil packet in her face.

Satisfied, she wound her fingers tightly in Sloan's hair and used her grip to pull him back down. "Now where were we?"

The water handler laughed but returned to his explorations easily.

He feasted on her forever, sucking and nipping at her sensitive skin until she could barely remember her own name. She was sure her body would be littered with hickies and the occasional bite mark, but she didn't care. What he was doing felt too damn good to stop and besides, it wasn't like everyone in the castle didn't already know they were sleeping together.

She was far from still. She arched, shifted, in an attempt to get closer. She clawed at his back when he kissed a particularly responsive spot. She pulled at his hair when she wanted him to repeat something. "Enough." She was afraid she would burst into flames if he didn't get in her soon.

Instead of crawling between her thighs, like she expected, Sloan rolled off her and urged her up. "On your hands and knees, baby. I want to take you from behind."

A bolt of electricity shot to her clit as she obeyed his order. She hadn't been a virgin when she'd met Sloan, and she'd done more than missionary sex before, but something about being taken like that by Sloan was enough to set her dancing on the fine edge of orgasm.

Almost instantly, she felt him nudging at her pussy. She pushed back so the tip of his shaft popped in. A moan worked its way up her throat, and she started rocking back and forth, too impatient to wait for him to move. The position made him feel bigger, thicker, and taking him like that bordered on pain. But the small bite of discomfort only served to highlight the pleasure she felt.

He moved slowly, and she groaned with frustration.

She wanted to feel him pound into her with a raw urgency that told her how much he needed her. "Faster," she demanded.

The hands on her hips tightened. "The lady's wish is my command," he said before drastically increasing his pace.

Her fingers scrabbled at the ground as she tried to steady herself. Her lust wound tighter, spiraling impossibly higher. She needed something ... more. "Sloan," she cried, tossing her head.

He let out a sound, part groan, part growl, and she looked over her shoulder at him. His head was bent, and he concentrated fiercely on something. She gasped when she realized he was watching his dick slide in and out of her body. How hot was that? "Sunny," he said through gritted teeth. "I'm close, sweetheart. I need you to come now."

"I can't," she wailed. "I'm so close but ... I can't."

She was beyond herself. She had no idea what she needed, but apparently Sloan knew.

He slid one hand from her hip around to her front and ground his finger against her clit. The dual sensation of having him in her and on her broke through her wall, and she tumbled into orgasm.

It was spectacular. Her entire body throbbed, and Sloan never slowed, letting her ride her orgasm right to the end. Finally, he froze and his cock kicked inside her. She could feel the pulse of his release into the condom, and it wrung yet another small orgasm from her electrified body.

When it was over and she was sure she could still feel her legs, she found herself face down on the grass, fighting to draw enough oxygen into her lungs to survive. "Holy shit," she whispered. "That was fantastic."

"Fan-fucking-tastic," Sloan agreed.

They lay there for a few minutes. "Hey, Sloan? Can you magic our clothes back, please? I'd rather not walk back to the car with my bare ass hanging out."

A look of horror crossed his face. She suddenly had a bad feeling. "Sloan?" she said, trying to make her tone as ominous as possible. "Don't joke about things like this."

She relaxed when he smiled. "Just kidding. Well, not really. I can't make them come back. I never figured out how to reverse the spell. It was a miracle I even learned the part that I did. We handlers aren't known for our magical abilities outside of manipulating our element."

She opened her mouth to shriek at him when he held his hand up. "I sort of hoped this would happen one day, so—" he crawled over to a hollow tree—"I hid a change of clothes for both of us a couple of days ago."

The sweatpants he handed her pooled around her ankles, and she positively swam in the T-shirt. Of course, he hadn't thought to bring shoes. There was also a conspicuous lack of underwear, but she had a feeling the last omission was on purpose.

Everyone would know what they had been up to, but it was better than sneaking back into the castle like a teenager.

He put his arm around her shoulders and tugged her close. "Come on."

The happy smile on his face dispelled any misgivings she had about the wardrobe choices he'd made. It was really the first time he'd looked so happy, so carefree, since she'd met him.

Wrapping her arm around his waist, she let him lead her toward the car. She was determined to do whatever it took to keep that look on his face for as long as he would have her.

Chapter Twenty-two

Since their dinner of macaroni and alfredo sauce, Sloan had taken to arranging little surprised for her. Sometimes, a single rose would be waiting on her dresser when she got to her room.

Once, he'd arranged for them to have cooking lessons at one of the restaurants in town.

Twice, she'd come to dinner to find a newly released book she'd been talking about. Then he'd read it with her.

Tonight, he'd surprised her with a midnight picnic. He'd parked at a clearing about forty-five minutes away from the castle, just so they could have some, "extra privacy."

The night was beautiful. There wasn't a cloud in the sky, the moon was full and the stars looked like diamonds pinned to black velvet. It was perfect for a romantic picnic.

Sunny guessed the ideal evening was the reason Sloan had decided they should blow off their training and do something fun instead.

She was quite impressed with his plans. He'd packed a huge wicker basket with all her favorite finger goods. There were chocolate dipped strawberries, tiny squares of brownies, fruit tarts and even a tin of peanut brittle. It was nutritionally lacking, but so what? The bottle of champagne made up for it. At least, that's what she told herself.

A cool berry pressed to her lips and she opened her mouth, accepting the treat. "Having fun?" Sloan asked, wiping away a bit of juice that had escaped the corner of her mouth with his thumb.

She nodded as she swallowed. "I am, thanks. It's nice not to have to think about magic for a few minutes."

Sloan shifted until their shoulders were touching and played with the ends of her hair. "You've been working so hard. I thought you deserved a break."

"Well, you're a great teacher. I can't believe how much I'm able to control my power now."

Sloan smiled proudly. "You're doing great. God, I love you so much," he blurted.

Her throat tightened, and she looked away from him. It hurt, not being able to give him back those three words. Because she was in love with him. Deeply and completely. But the fear of losing him was lodged too deeply into her heart. What hurt most was the fact she knew that in order to be with him, she needed to let go of her fear. But knowing it and doing it were two entirely different things.

Sloan, apparently catching on to her distress, sighed and tugged on her hand until she had no choice but to stretch out on the blanket they'd laid on the grass. "Let's not think too hard," he said as he sprawled next to her.

It was the best idea she'd heard all day. She scooted closer to Sloan's warm body and rested her head on his outstretched arm so she could stare up at the night sky. Lazily, she raised her hand and started tracing shapes in the air with her fire. "How long can you hold the fire there?" he asked.

Smiling, she wrote Sloan's full name in the air, making the flames burn much brighter than normal. She traced two little hearts on either side of his name and forced them to flare red. Maybe she wasn't ready to voice her love, but she could at least show him a little.

She held the flame for a full minute before letting it flicker out, only to write his name again and enclose it in a giant heart.

Sloan laughed and kissed the top of her head. Reaching straight up, he summoned a palm full of water and threw it in the air, manipulating it so it also held the shape of a heart.

They played until the wee hours of the morning, giggling like little kids and stopping to make out every once in a while.

Finally sitting up, Sunny stretched her arms and shoulders. "This was so much fun. Thank you for tonight."

Sloan sat up beside her and kissed her temple. "Well, hopefully, we'll have many more nights like this in the future. No pressure," he added with a sheepish smile.

"Just give me time," she whispered.

He nodded and stood up. "We should get going. Raven's going to want us to train tomorrow afternoon, so we should get a couple of hours of sleep at least."

"That slave driver," she joked, standing up and brushing off the seat of her jeans.

Sloan waggled his eyebrows at her and cupped her hips. "Want some help?"

She pushed him off with a laugh and bent down to pack up the basket. "You're insatiable."

"What?" he asked in an innocent voice. "I haven't had you since this morn..."

The frisson of unease that shot up her spine told her exactly why Sloan had trailed off. "What is that?" She could hear the fear in her voice.

Sloan looked around carefully and her uneasiness increased dramatically. "We're sensing a sudden increase in the amount of magic around us."

"Could it be Anna or Raven coming to look for us?" she asked. She already knew the answer, but was hopeful Sloan's would be different than what she expected.

Sloan starting tossing things into the basket with much more haste than he'd taken them out. "No. Any magic coming from a MacAlister witch would be recognizable. This magic is pretty unfamiliar. I've only encountered it a couple of times."

He didn't have to say where he'd encountered it. She could already sense the familiarity of the magic. It brought her back to the pub. The Takahashi handler was somewhere nearby. And the amount of magic crackling in the air told her he probably wasn't alone. "Let's leave the stuff," she said urgently. "We can come back for it later if anybody really cares about it."

The magic nearby increased and Sunny was surprised she didn't see sparks flying. It felt like she was pushing through a static field. The fine hairs on her arms stood on end.

"Fuck it," Sloan said, abandoning the basket. "I'll buy a new one if anyone misses it that badly."

"We should call Raven before we leave," she said.

Sloan grimaced. "Did you bring your phone?"

She shook her head. "I left it in my room. I didn't think I'd need it."

Grimacing again, Sloan sighed. "I was holding out hope you'd brought yours. I left mine in the car."

"God, we're so stupid," she said.

Sloan took a deep breath and shook his hands. "There's nothing we can do about it now. Besides, Raven and Leith will probably feel the increase of magic too. Let's go."

They made their way as silently as possible through the field, but there was little to give them any type of camouflage. "Maybe we should get down on our hands and knees?" she suggested. "The grass might be tall enough in some parts to hide us."

Sloan considered it for a second but quickly shook his head. "I think we need to focus on speed. Besides, I can't see them."

Sunny didn't bother to point out that it was the middle of the night. She grabbed his hand and quickened her speed. "How did they find us?"

Sloan shrugged and grabbed her hand, tugging her along behind him. "We didn't do anything major with our magic, but we did use it a lot," he said. "Maybe they tracked it, and because we're so far away from the castle, they decided to try and ambush us."

She cursed herself for playing with her flame so much to amuse Sloan. She'd drawn pictures in the air with it for close to three hours. "I'm sorry," she said.

Sloan shook his head but didn't look at her. He was too busy scanning their surroundings. "If it's anyone's fault, it's mine. I knew the Takahashi handler was in the country, and I still brought you here."

She didn't say anything, not because she agreed with him, but because his car, which they'd left at the side of the road, came into view. The fact that they had yet to see anyone was more than a little creepy. It felt like they were being hunted by some kind of top tier predator. Was this what a deer felt like when it was being stalked by a wolf?

"Just a little farther to go," Sloan whispered.

It could never be that easy, of course. As soon as they were within sprinting distance, a lone figure stood up from where he'd been crouched by the hood of the car. He lifted the car in the air and spun it around. "It took you long enough," he said casually, as though lifting a car with his mind was a daily occurrence. Then again, maybe it was.

"We're in so much shit," Sloan murmured.

"Yes," the handler agreed, and threw the car at them.

Sunny summoned as much fire as she could, hoping to melt the entire car before it hit them. Getting hit with a mass of melted metal wasn't much better than getting hit by a solid piece of metal, but at least she was doing something.

Sloan, however, beat her to the punch. He summoned a jet of water strong enough to push the car off track so it hit the ground to the right of them with a deafening crash.

Frustrated, scared and angry, Sunny lost control of her temper. "What the hell is it with you and cars?" she screamed.

Despite the situation, Sloan started laughing. What was more startling was the fact that the Takahashi handler started laughing too. "I wish you were a Takahashi," he called. "I bet life is never boring with you around."

"She's mine," Sloan growled, his chuckles disappearing immediately.

Sunny frowned, a little unsure as to what was going on. Were they seriously having a pissing contest? And, she would really have to have a talk with Sloan about the whole "she's mine" thing.

The Takahashi handler's laughter died too. "It's a shame we have to say good-bye. I think we could have been good friends if we'd been in a different situation."

"Why are you doing this?" Sunny asked, stalling for time. Hopefully, Leith had felt the same surge of power and was already on his way.

"You really have to ask?" the Takahashi shouted, a sudden fury contorting his features.

Sunny risked a glance at Sloan and realized he was as confused as she was. "Forgive me for wanting to know why you're attempting to murder us," she sneered. Once again, fear had taken control of her tongue. She doubted very much that the Takahashi handler would be as for-giving as Leith.

"You killed our leader," he spat. "Do you know what happens to handlers when their leader dies?"

The answer was not the one she was expecting. And she had no idea what losing a leader would do a handler.

Judging by Sloan's horrified gasp, he knew. "We didn't kill her," Sloan responded. Sunny felt Sloan's hand clamp down on her elbow and he tugged her, none too gently, until she pressed against his side.

The Takahashi grew more manic, his movements wild and the expression more terrifying. "We smelled MacAl-ister magic. Like I said, it's too bad the young one wasn't a Takahashi. She would have been spared."

"What is he talking about?" Sunny whispered.

"You know how Raven's set up some spells to help dampen our magic so we can sleep without fear of losing control?" Sloan answered, keeping a wary eye on the other handler.

"Yeah."

"Only a clan leader can do that. Until another leader has come forward, handlers cannot get any safe rest. They tend to go mad without their leaders. It's an unspo-ken rule that the leaders are left alone, or at least alive, or else the damage a clan's handlers will create will be cata-strophic."

"That would have been a good thing to mention ear-lier," she hissed. Why did she always have to learn about the bad stuff in an emergency?

"Exactly," the handler replied as if praising a student. "So you'll understand if I'm just crazy enough to start the war early."

At the handler's sudden nod, a sudden wave of people and wolves surrounded them. They seemed to appear out of thin air. Swearing under his breath, Sloan threw up a water shield. They were completely surrounded on all sides by a wall of water.

"Where did they come from?" Sunny asked, stunned.

Sloan didn't look particularly surprised, but he did look wary. "It's one of the Takahashi's specialties. They can conceal their presence somewhat. We could feel them but couldn't see them."

Any other time, Sunny would have been amazed and fascinated. Right then, she was far too scared. "And the wolves?"

"Probably the Takahashis' allies, the wolf shifters. Sit tight, Raven and the others should be here soon. There's no way they didn't feel my magic surge."

The wavy outline of the Takahashis and the wolves on the other side of the shield Sloan had erected showed they were slowly approaching. "Will they be able to get through the water?"

"Saying it would be uncomfortable would be an understatement, but yes, if they try hard enough, they can get through."

Sloan's eyes never left the shield, but she knew what he was thinking. She needed to join her power with his if they wanted to survive. But he wouldn't ask because he knew how much she disliked feeling vulnerable to him.

One of the wolves approached the wall of water and stuck a paw into it. She could hear the wolf's yelp over the rushing water, but the paw broke through the shield.

She shot a ball of fire at the wolf's paw and the wolf withdrew it from their little space.

Sunny's eyes teared up. She was prepared to die, and she was okay with it. What she wasn't okay with was Sloan dying. Especially if she hadn't done everything in her power to save him.

Taking a deep breath, Sunny focused on Sloan's magic

and opened herself—body, mind, and soul—to him.

Chapter Twenty-three

Sunny knew the second Sloan figured out what she was trying to do. His eyes widened and she figured he'd gotten a sense of how deeply she loved him. But it wasn't how she wanted to say the words so she stayed quiet.

Wordlessly, she wove her magic with Sloan's and a sudden understanding sparked in her brain. Her magic didn't require a calm, focused mind to control it. It responded to passion. She needed to let go of everything she'd been holding back and let that passion control the flames.

Instead of forming fire, Sunny found herself led to something entirely different. She decided to go for it and followed her instincts. "Can you hold the shield and make it rain at the same time?" she asked.

Eyes wide, Sloan nodded. "This is something we've never tried, Sunny. Even the previous fire handler didn't know how to do that."

The fact that he knew what she thought was pretty damn cool. She could feel his admiration and support through their temporary bond. Maybe being connected with this man on all levels wouldn't be so bad. If she could trust him to support her when she was thinking of doing something so crazy, then she could trust him with her feelings.

"I know what I'm doing. I think," she answered. "Can you hold it?"

He nodded and it started to rain. "I can hold this for as long as you need."

"Good." Hopefully she wouldn't need him to hold

things for long. Raven, Anna and Leith should already be on their way. If she could inflict enough damage, she should be able to hold off the attacks long enough.

A sudden understanding of her magic had swept her. She couldn't create fire from nothing. But she could manipulate the temperature of any molecule, causing it to erupt into flame.

To test her theory, she focused on one particular drop of rain and willed it to heat up. Within seconds, she had created a drop of steam.

Would it work the same if she willed the heat out of it?

Instantly, the flame extinguished and the water re-formed.

Concentrating intently, she drew the remaining heat from the water until it was nothing but ice.

Victory rushed through her bloodstream and she risked a glance up at Sloan. "Did you see that?"

He nodded. "Yes. You'll have to tell me how you did it later." She could tell he left out the, *if we survive* part.

She unleashed her anger, letting the hot rage rush through her. Her magic responded to her passion and she focused the energy on the raindrops Sloan created. Instead of summoning fire, she concentrated on the water itself, lowering the temperature of the liquid. Sloan hummed his approval and manipulated the shape of the quickly freezing drops into daggers. He flung them at the offending witches and she smiled darkly when she heard a cry of pain. Apparently, Sloan had really good aim.

The ice daggers slowed down the attacks but didn't stop them. A tree branch crashed through their shield and just about took her head off. Wolves were hurling themselves at the wall of rushing water, sometimes succeeding in breaking through for a few seconds before Sunny was able to shoot a fireball at them.

She lost her temper again when a wolf broke through and nearly managed to close his jaws on the man she loved. Splitting her concentration in half, she continued to freeze the drops of rain even as she superheated the water shield so the water boiled as it fell.

Her efforts helped with the wolves but didn't do anything against the debris the Takahashi handler kept hurling at them. "Where the hell is everyone?" she screamed.

Sloan squinted through the steamy water shield. "There's some kind of attack from behind," he said.

She strained her eyes, trying to see through both the water and the crowd of witches and wolves. Now that she knew the key to controlling her magic, she didn't have a problem continuing to hold her attack. "I can hardly see them," she cried over the din. "Why wouldn't Anna help us fry these suckers?"

Sloan's eyes narrowed. "I'm not sure. But we need to hold them off until then."

Another chunk of metal came flying through the shield. It missed Sloan's leg by a scant inch. "That's it," she screamed. She let her magic take over, giving it free rein.

What happened shocked even her.

Fire shot out of the shield, attaching itself to the falling rain. Instead of turning the water into steam, it turned the drops into flames.

It was raining fire.

"Holy shit," Sloan screamed over the noise.

With another shift in focus, she was able to hold the fiery rain, as well as continue to hold the temperature of the shield and draw out the heat from certain drops so they were still able to use the ice daggers.

The immense amount of energy it took to hold all

three took its toll though, and she felt her energy starting to flag. "I don't know how much longer I can handle this," she said to Sloan.

"I don't think you'll have to," Sloan shouted. "It looks like they're retreating. They're still being attacked from behind."

Sloan's last words were said a little roughly, almost as if he didn't like what was happening. "What the matter?" she asked.

"I'm pretty sure they're being attacked by hunters. I guess it was too much to hope they wouldn't be alerted by the commotion."

Well, so much for hoping they were in the clear. "Do you think if we stop now, we can slip out in the commotion?"

Sloan shook his head. "No. The water shield is pretty obvious. If we drop it, it will be noticed and if the Takahashis don't attack us again, the hunters will."

Her energy was draining rapidly, and with it, her ability to keep the three different strands of her magic powered. She'd never run into a problem where she'd drained her magic but, then again, she'd never pushed it this hard before. Her knees buckled and she sank to the ground. The raining fire and ice daggers disappeared and the water rushing around them went from boiling to lukewarm. "Sorry," she whispered.

"Don't worry, sweetheart." Sloan took over the defense, letting the shield fall since it was doing nothing to keep out the arrows and bullets the hunters were shooting at them.

She watched, dazed and exhausted, as he started sweeping hunters away with jets of water. The Takahashis and their allies were in full retreat, taking their dead and injured with them. She struggled to her feet and started summoning as many small balls of fire as she could. She couldn't send them far, but at least if one of the hunters got too close, she could do *something* instead of just sitting there.

There were too many hunters, though, and as hard as they tried, they weren't able to keep all of them away.

Finally, a familiar car came into view. Raven, Anna and Leith jumped out.

The arrival of their saviors caught her attention and was the distraction the hunters needed, and a horrible pain in her stomach had her doubling over. She clutched at her abdomen, her hands closing around an arrow.

Sunny fell again, only barely managing to roll onto her back instead of driving the arrow deeper into her gut.

The last thing she saw before passing out was the look of horror on Sloan's face.

*

Sloan's heart stopped when the hunter shot Sunny in the stomach with her crossbow. A rage like he'd never experienced swept through him. A giant wave, bigger than anything he'd ever summoned, formed, totally without his consent. It crashed over the hunters, sweeping them away and completely out of sight. He had enough control over the wave to make sure it parted around Raven, Anna and Leith, but he'd probably drowned the hunters. And he didn't care.

He dropped to his knees next to Sunny and seized her hand. "Sunny?" he choked out. "Sweetheart?"

Her eyes seemed larger than ever in her pale face. She blinked up at him, but didn't say anything. She didn't even seem to be aware of her surroundings.

He pressed his lips to her knuckles. He couldn't lose her. But there was nothing he could do for her at the moment. "Raven," he screamed, knowing his leader was on his way. "Raven! Sunny's been hurt."

"On it," Raven called back, running at full speed toward them.

Sloan could see Leith pulling out his phone and pressing it to his ear. Anna started prowling around, falling back into their training from years ago and making sure they were covered in case of another attack.

He resisted the urge to gather Sunny up in his arms for fear of doing her further damage. He clutched her hand tighter and held it to his heart. "Sunny, don't leave me. Please, baby, I'm begging you. Fight, sweetheart."

Her eyes started to glaze over and her breathing began to slow. "No," he screamed, squeezing her hand. "Don't let go. I need you."

It didn't matter how hard he pleaded with her. Her breathing continued to slow and became shallower with each inhale. Desperate, Sloan sent his magic out, looking for hers. It was there, faint and dim, but it was there. He tugged on her magic, drawing it up and strengthening it with his. "Sunny Kerrigan," he said firmly. "You are going to live. I love you, and I can't live through the death of my soul mate. So, hold it together."

Raven came skidding to a stop next to him and dropped to his knees. "Oh, fuck," he whispered. The leader's hands hovered over her stomach, but he didn't actually touch her. "Hold on, Sunny. The paramedics are on their way." Sure enough, sirens were floating on the air, their shrill sound reassuring.

Sloan ignored the man and focused his full attention on the woman bleeding on the road. She was blinking at him again, only this time he could see the question on her face. "Sunny," he said, just to make sure she knew he was talking to and about her. "Dara will always have a place in my heart. But I love you. *You.* I never thought I'd be able to love someone as passionately as I love you. You dragged me back into the land of the living. If you die ... well, Raven will have to kill me because I'll go on a rampage without you."

Talk about putting pressure on someone. He didn't say anything else. He held her hand, terrified that if he let go, she would float away from him.

The paramedics finally pulled up and jumped out of the ambulance. He could hear what they were saying, but he didn't understand a single word. All he knew was that someone was trying to pull him away from his Sunny.

He fought tooth and nail to stay with her, but strong arms wrapped around him from behind. "Let them work, lad," Leith said lowly.

Sloan stopped fighting, but Leith didn't remove his arms, for which Sloan was grateful. "Damn hunters," he spat.

"Hunters did this?" one of the paramedics asked while they were securing Sunny to the stretcher.

"Aye," Leith said. "We've had a group of them using strange weapons to hunt rabbits late at night."

The paramedic frowned. "Have you reported this to the police?"

Raven shook his head. "No. We didn't really know who to contact."

Why were these daft paramedics questioning who shot Sunny? Their job was to take her to the hospital, and keep her alive on the way. Luckily for them, they started loading her into the ambulance before he could unleash his tongue. Raven turned to them. "I'll ride with Sunny. Leith, you bring Sloan and Anna."

Sloan knew there was no use arguing. As rich and powerful as Raven was, as well as the fact that he made very regular, very generous donations to the hospital, meant that the man had a lot of influence. The hospital would probably bend over backward to try and please him.

Anna rushed over with the car keys in hand. "Luckily you didn't wash Raven's car away. Are you okay?" she asked, inspecting him critically for injury.

He couldn't keep it in anymore. His eyes filled with tears, and he didn't even attempt to hide them. They fell down his face unchecked. "She can't die," he whispered.

Leith turned him around and cupped the back of his head. Sloan found himself with his face suddenly smashed into the bigger man's chest. He was stunned. In all the time he'd known Leith, the man had never offered anyone such comfort. Not even after Dara's death, had he offered more than a small smile. And here he was, obviously aware of how much he loved Sunny, and literally offered Sloan a shoulder to cry on.

His body gave in, and he let his friend bear most of his weight as he sobbed.

Chapter Twenty-four

It had been a long, hard road to recovery for Sunny. When she'd first woken up in the hospital room, she thought someone had died. All the occupants of MacAlister Castle had gathered in her room and looked as if they were at a funeral.

She'd lost a kidney and her spleen to the hunter's arrow and had been in a considerable amount of pain for weeks. Even now, six months later, her wound still tugged and twinged occasionally.

But she and Sloan were both alive, and that's all that mattered.

Sloan had brought her home three weeks after the attack, and had been waiting on her hand and foot ever since then.

She laid still, savoring the heavy warmth of the blankets. Winter had hit Scotland hard, and it was damn cold, even to her Canadian blood.

The sound of birds filled the airy room and a puddle of sunlight splashed over Sunny's face. She groaned and rolled over, burying her face into the pillow. "Too early," she complained. Why had they left the curtains open last night? Oh, right. They'd been too hot for each other to bother worrying about them last night.

Reaching out one arm, Sunny searched for the warm body that was usually sprawled out next to her. She frowned when she failed to find him. Muttering grumpily, she turned her head and cracked one eye open.

Sloan was nowhere in sight. But if the sound of running water, and the deep voice singing cheerily from the bathroom were any indication, Sloan was in the shower.

She pouted at the fact she didn't wake up in Sloan's arms.

But Sloan in the shower was a pretty good compromise. A naked, wet and happy Sloan, if the tune he was singing was any indication, was always a good thing. Add that to the fact he could do some pretty awesome things with the water in the shower, and she was in for a good time.

With that thought in mind, Sunny bounced out of bed and sauntered over to the bathroom. The steam hung thick in the air when she walked in. Sloan had switched to whistling, and she shook her head. He whistled "Yankee Doodle," something he'd taken to doing when she insisted on some good, old-fashioned American food when she'd been in the hospital.

She smiled at the memory. She had been cranky, in pain and completely sick of hospital food. She'd demanded a burger, fries and chocolate shake. He'd been happy to run out and get her what she wanted, but she'd insisted on the meal coming from McDonald's. There was exactly one McDonald's in the immediate area, about twenty minutes' drive from the hospital. She'd really enjoyed that meal though.

"Are you coming or what?" Sloan called from the shower.

"Yeah, yeah," she answered. She slipped into the stall with him and shut the door again, enclosing them in the steamy air. "Hi."

Sloan flashed a bright grin and smoothed her hair back from her face. "You were drooling on my shoulder this morning," he teased.

Still slightly grumpy because she hadn't woken up to some lazy morning loving, she stuck her tongue out at him, but didn't stop him when his soapy hands slid down her belly. He paused when he got to the scar, his hands hovering over it protectively.

When she'd first seen the scar, she'd been horrified. It was huge and ugly and had made her cry every time she looked at it. But Sloan had soothed her ruffled feathers. He'd been insistent that the scar wasn't ugly. It was only a reminder of how hard she'd fought to stay alive, and he said he found it sexy.

He'd proved his words over and over. There hadn't been a day since she'd come home that he hadn't worshiped the spot with his lips. And today was no exception. He dropped to his knees and kissed her stomach gently.

She twined his wet hair around her fingers and shivered when he trailed his lips over her sensitive hip bone. "Sloan," she moaned when he stayed where he was, just teasing.

"Don't worry, babe. We'll get there."

"But when?" she whined.

Sloan pushed himself to his feet and loomed over her. "My baby doesn't feel like waiting today?"

She shook her head and wrapped one leg around his thigh, grinding her pussy against his hard muscles. Some days, she loved foreplay. And the good lord knew, Sloan was a master at foreplay.

But there were other days, like today, where she wanted it hard and fast.

"What my lady wants, my lady gets," Sloan said with a lascivious wink. He slid his hand between her legs and tested her readiness. "Oh, baby. God, you're so wet."

Gripping her hips, Sloan yanked her away from his thigh and spun her around so she was facing the shower wall. The motion was so quick, she had to slap her hands against the wall to keep her balance.

Yes. She absolutely loved when he took her like this.

He slid into her without hesitation, until his balls were resting against her thighs. "Fuck, sweetheart," he groaned, pulling out and sinking back in. "I'm not going to last long."

She, however, was nowhere near ready to climax. If they had been anywhere but the shower, she would have dropped her hand to her sex and fingered her clit, just to catch up with him.

Sloan seemed to know exactly what she needed. She squealed when she felt a tiny jet of water begin to pummel the exquisitely sensitive right side of her clit.

The orgasm hit her unexpectedly and her inner muscles clenched around him. Sloan kept the water in place even as he pounded into her and her climax seemed to go on forever.

By the time they'd recovered enough to move, the water had gone cold. Wrapped in large, fluffy towels, they stumbled over to the bed and collapsed. "Good morning," he said.

Smiling, she extracted one of her arms, which had become tangled in the blankets, and poked him in the side. "Say it," she said instead of wishing him a good morning.

This time it was Sloan's turn to stick out his tongue. "Why do I have to be the first one to say it?"

She poked him again. "Because you owe me."

Sloan's eyebrows flew up and he stared at her incredulously. "For what?"

Oh, Sloan was going to love this. "For dragging you back into the land of the living."

Sloan rolled his eyes and propped himself up on his elbows. "You're never going to let me live that down, are you?"

She planned on never forgetting those words. They were what had kept her going when all she wanted to do was let go of the pain and fade away. But she wasn't going to tell him that. He already had a big enough ego. "Tell me," she said again.

Letting out a very exasperated breath, Sloan rested his chin on one of his palms. "Fine. I love you. I love you with every breath I take and every beat of my heart. Happy now?"

She could have done without the sarcasm, but she knew he was just messing with her. "Very. Sloan?"

Sloan snorted but softened it with a smile. "Yeah?"

"I love you, too."

Rolling on to his back, Sloan put his arms behind his head and smiled up at the ceiling, looking entirely too pleased with the situation. "I know."

Huffing, Sunny looked up at the ceiling too, and crossed her arms over her chest. "You're such a know-it-all."

The mattress dipped, and Sloan hovered over her. "I *do* know it all. For example, I know if I do this, you'll be all over me in seconds." He nibbled on her neck, sending new sparks through her body to collect between her legs.

She wrapped her arms around his neck and pulled him close. "I love that you're a know it all," she whispered, shivering when his hand dipped between her legs to play gently with her clit.

He smiled softly and kissed the corner of her mouth. "I love you so much," he said quietly.

She pushed a lock of hair off his forehead and looked into his face. "I love you too."

Chapter Twenty-five

Five Months Later

Raven nibbled at his dessert, savoring the rich taste of the chocolate cake as he looked around the dining room. Leith sat by the fireplace, scowling into his drink. He'd been like that for weeks now, ever since Matthew had been released from the hospital.

Sunny and Sloan were sitting half-way down the table in their own little world. They were bickering over something, occasionally sending little bursts of magic aimed at the other. The effect was ruined by the fact that they stopped to kiss every other second.

They were a welcome distraction from everything else going on. He'd talked to Prince Gareth about the Takahashi's accusation. The prince had taken advantage of his numerous contacts and had confirmed the Takahashi leader really had been murdered. And without a leader, the handlers had to be going more than slightly mad by now. The problem was that leaders didn't come along every day. A leader was born. Usually they were identified before the death of the leader and trained. It wasn't like any old witch could stand up and be a clan leader.

Worse yet, the rumor floating around whispered that the Takahashi handler had been, if not married to the leader, at least in a very intimate relationship with her. If the rumor was true, it was amazing the Takahashi handler hadn't destroyed the whole damn world.

He'd managed to get word through a very trusted source to the Keita clan that the Takahashi leader had been slain. He'd received a response back that the Keita clan would increase their leader's security.

As for any MacAlister involvement in the murder, he really couldn't say. He'd been apart from his clan members for so long, he was afraid he'd lost his hold on them. He'd discussed the possibility at length with Leith, but neither of them could really figure out how to determine the truth.

But if someone was killing clan leaders, he really needed to step up the search for the next MacAlister leader. Because if he died, there would be nothing to stop his handlers from shaking the whole damn world apart in their sleep. Or causing a flood of biblical proportions. Or burning the whole damn thing to the core.

Blinking his eyes, he pushed the thoughts away and turned his attention back to Sunny and Sloan. Sloan lifted his fork, offering her a bite of his crème brulee. He smiled at them even though they weren't even giving him the time of day. It was nice to have some happiness back in the castle. Hopefully soon, they would have even more laughter. "So, what do you think we should do about the influx of clan members coming in?" he asked Anna, picking up the conversation they'd dropped to watch Sunny and Sloan.

She pursed her lips and tapped her fork lightly against her plate. "Well, the cottages on the property are still in good shape. They just need some updating. And there's plenty of room in the castle. Maybe we can give families the cottages and have the singles and couples stay here in the castle?"

Raven nodded, trying to imagine the quiet castle alive with people. It had been just the five of them for so long, he'd almost forgotten what it was like to have people everywhere, singing, laughing and bickering. When was the last time he'd held a baby? It had always been one of his favorite parts of having his clan with him. The kids.

Of course, there were going to be a lot more people living here than ever before very shortly. Not every clan member had resided in Scotland before the war. Some, like Matthew's family, had made their homes elsewhere and only traveled to Scotland for the annual clan meeting. Now, with the decision to call each and every clan member to the castle, he had to figure out a way to house and feed all these people efficiently. Money wasn't the issue. He had more than enough. He'd been blessed with the ability to understand fluctuating markets and knew exactly when and where to invest and when to sell.

"That's a good idea," he said to Anna. "Do you know anyone who could help get the cottages ready?"

Anna had taken over calling the clan members when Matthew had started negotiating alliance terms with the dragons, but her real talent was event planning. If anyone knew how to get things done, it was Anna.

Thankfully, Anna nodded. "I do. Let me make some calls, and I'll have people here by the day after tomorrow. We'll probably have to look into doing some work in the castle too. Only two of the wings are being used right now. The other three haven't really been touched in probably thirty years, at least."

"Okay. Just let me know what I have to do."

Anna smiled and popped another bit of dessert into her mouth. Sunny chose that moment to set Sloan's crème brulee on fire in a small display of magic. Instead of yelling, Sloan blew the flame out and took a bite. "Mmm," he said, offering Sunny a bite.

"They're kind of sickening, aren't they?" Anna said softly, gesturing to the couple with her fork.

Raven smiled sadly. He remembered the times when he and Niya would play like that. "It's nice to see a little bit of love though, isn't it?" he responded.

Anna patted his arm. "Don't worry. You'll find her."

Stunned, Raven stared at Anna for a few seconds before shifting his gaze to his plate. He'd always wondered if Anna had known about his relationship with the dragon queen. He remembered the looks she used to toss him, those little knowing smiles, when he'd talk about the dragons. But she'd never said anything, and he'd eventually dismissed the idea as him being paranoid.

Raven was saved from responding by Matthew, who came hobbling in, back from his meeting with Prince Gareth. "Hi," Matthew said brightly as he let his cane drop to the floor and sat in the chair next to Raven.

"Hi, yourself." Raven raised an eyebrow at the young man's appearance. He was flushed and the silly smile wouldn't leave his face. His hair was ruffled and his normally impeccable suit was wrinkled. In short, Matthew looked like he'd been ravished. Raven couldn't help but wonder about the logistics of having sex with Matthew's bad leg. But clearly, Matthew and Gareth had figured it out just fine.

Matthew grabbed Raven's fork and helped himself to a chunk of cake. "Yum," he said.

Anna laughed and pushed her own cake over to Matthew, who looked at her with a delighted expression. "Do you want me to get you some dinner?" Anna offered.

Mouth full, Matthew shook his head. He swallowed before talking. "No, thanks. Gareth fed me. I just felt like something a little sweet."

Raven glanced over at Leith in time to see him slam back a drink before getting up to prowl around the room. He mentally shook his head. He couldn't figure Leith out. One second he treated Matthew like a little brother, the next, he pouted when Matthew found someone who was interested in him. Did the man return Matthew's feelings or was he just jealous because now the younger man had seemed to put aside his hero worship and was spending time with someone else instead of following him like a puppy?

Matthew's smile had dimmed a little when Raven turned around again. He presented Raven with a sheaf of papers and attacked Anna's cake with what Raven recognized to be forced enthusiasm. "The negotiations went well. Basically, as long as we make a genuine effort to help in the search for the queen, the dragons will fight by our side whether we've found her or not. But Gareth included some reports on where the dragons have searched and where they suspect she might be being held. That's why there are so many papers."

Raven pushed his cake closer to Matthew, knowing the boy would eat it all, and shuffled through the papers, concentrating on the reports Matthew had mentioned. He was more hopeful he'd find his love now than he had been in years. *I promise, Niya. I will rescue you.*

He flipped a page and felt a tingle run up his arm. He froze as a giant wave of power rushed over him.

The power was still radiating through him when he finally managed to move his eyes and search the room for the seeker. Leith had gone rigid and a look of intense concentration was on his face.

"The earth handler has come into his magic."

Raven shot to his feet. "Find him, Leith. Before the Takahashis do."

The End

ABOUT THE AUTHOR

Lynn lives in Ontario, Canada with her husband and children. She spends her days writing about werewolves and vampires, and longs for a pet unicorn of her own. You can find Lynn at:
www.lynntylerbooks.com or on Facebook

www.ingramcontent.com/pod-product-compliance
Lightning Source LLC
Chambersburg PA
CBHW032116170626
46808CB00006B/1969